WHEN'S IT DUE, SOPHIE DREW?

KATEY LOVELL

Print ISBN 978-1-914614-04-0

ALSO BY KATEY LOVELL

Nothing New for Sophie Drew

For all the anxious over-thinkers

DECEMBER

CHAPTER 1

There it was, squirming on the screen. A grainy grey-white jelly baby, an actual little person nestling in my womb, tucked behind my already-expanding stomach and the three iced fingers I'd made Max pull over at Greggs to buy – not for me, for the baby, obviously.

My cheeks were damp, and I'd no chance of stopping the tears escaping as Max squeezed my hand – reassurance and love being sent through the pulse of his palm against mine – and said, "That's our baby."

Our baby.

Our. Baby.

No matter how many times I heard it, I still couldn't get my head around the fact there was a miniature human being in my stomach who, if the on-screen antics were anything to go by, was going to be as uncoordinated as me. Our baby (nope – still not used to it) looked like I do on the rare occasion I make it to Zumba class – arms and legs flailing in every direction.

"Is everything okay?" Max asked, and at first I thought he was talking to me, because I was still crying. "Is it the right size?"

I inhaled, the wait for the response feeling like forever.

"I need to take some more measurements," the lady replied evenly, tapping away on her computer touchpad, "but from what I've seen, Baby's looking around the right size for your dates."

My shoulders quivered, relief escaping through the hot tears that were in full flow. It wasn't long since my sister-in-law, Chantel, had had a stressful twin pregnancy, and although the sensible part of me knew I was doing all I could to be healthy – avoiding alcohol, eating a minimum of five pieces of fruit and veg a day, and not smoking (admittedly that last one hadn't been difficult, as I hadn't smoked since school, when my friend Tawna's mum had caught the pair of us leaning out of Tawna's bedroom window, taking turns to puff away on a shared Silk Cut) – there had still been a dark cloud of dread hanging over me in the build-up to the milestone scan, especially as I'd not found out I was pregnant until well into the second trimester. Not that the scan was a guarantee, of course, but seeing our unborn child wiggling around on the monitor reassured my overactive mind.

The sonographer pressed the wand firmly along my pubic line, the clear, cold gel she'd smothered across me earlier no match for her force. It was enough to make me regret at least two of the iced finger buns, and wish I'd not taken the instructions to drink a pint of water to heart. I was bursting for a wee, and what's more, it hurt.

I tightened my grip on Max's hand, and he let out a high-pitched noise somewhere between a squeak and a yelp. Anyone would think it was his liquid-filled stomach being violently probed with a phallic instrument that could see inside his body.

"Sorry if that's uncomfortable," the woman said, with not an ounce of apology evident in her jovial tone. "I'm trying to coax Baby to move a bit to get these last few measurements."

She pressed down harder still, and I breathed in sharply

through my teeth as I shifted my focus to counting the square tiles that formed the room's ceiling.

"Sophie's a warrior," Max said, and I wished I felt as sure of that fact as he sounded. It was all I could do to a) remember how to breathe and b) not wet myself, so I hardly felt like Princess Xena.

"I'm not sure about that," I managed, my voice snake-like through my gritted teeth.

"And we're done," she said with a smile, wiping her magic wand with a square of tissue. "Everything looks as it should at this stage, although the measurements suggest your dates are slightly out. Baby's measuring at eighteen weeks."

"Oh." A week less than the midwife had thought going on the date of my last period.

"That gives you a due date of May twenty-sixth," the sonographer said.

"He or she will be like me," Max said, "in the younger half of their year at school. I was always jealous of the kids who had their birthdays earlier in the year." His birthday, August the twenty-fifth, had meant he was the youngest in his year – his mum, Andrea, had told me how he'd cried on his seventh birthday because all his "friends" were either away on their jollies or forgot his party because it was so close to the end of the summer holidays.

"As long as this little one is fit and healthy, that's all that matters," I said, gladly taking the tissue offered me and wiping the excess gel from my stomach. Despite her efforts my knicker elastic was damp and sticky.

"Would you like photos to take away?"

I wondered if anyone who'd ever laid on that table had said, "Actually no, I'm not bothered." I doubt it. Whipping out the little card containing a shiny photo made up of every shade of the grey/black colour spectrum is the only way to make a pregnancy announcement. It's the law that you pass it around and everyone coos as they try to figure out which part of the ghostly outline is the head, and whether the long extension is an arm, a leg, the placenta, or if the baby in question is a super well-endowed boy (cue inappropriate jokes about whether or not they get that from Daddy).

"Yes please." Max grinned.

I kept my eyes fixed on the screen of the computer as I hoiked myself up to a sitting position. The swell of my stomach was barely-there, but there was definitely activity going on inside – for weeks it had felt as though my hips were being pulled apart. If it carried on I'd have snapped like a lucky Christmas wishbone by the time May rolled around.

The sonographer clicked her mouse on three different pictures and set them to print, reaching over to a stack of those oh-so-familiar cards. She cut the pictures down to size, popped them in the frames and told us the price. Max didn't hesitate in pulling the money out of his wallet ready to exchange for the photographs.

We said our "thank you"s and made it as far as the harshly lit corridor before scrabbling to look at the photos.

"I think it's got your nose," I said, cricking my neck to examine a picture of our baby's head in profile. "Look, it's that same little snub nose, I'm sure of it."

"That's our baby." Max reached out and wrapped his arm around my shoulder.

When I tore my eyes from the photographs and looked at my boyfriend, I noticed the tears in his eyes, glistening behind the thick lenses of his black-rimmed glasses.

"It is," I said, not quite able to believe it myself. "And I know we hadn't planned for things to happen this quickly, but I'm really, really glad they did." We'd been together less than a year when the digital test had surprised us with the word "pregnant", but we'd both been delighted at the thought of starting our much-wanted family.

"Me too. I love you, Sophie Drew, and I can't wait to meet our son or daughter."

"There's still another five months to go yet." I laughed and hugged my arms around his waist. The wool of his jumper tickled my fingertips. "You can't hurry cooking a baby."

"I can wait," he replied, his voice cracking with love. "It'll be more than worth it."

We took another moment to savour the photographs, mooning over how beautiful the tiny person we'd created was, before stepping out into the cool December sun. Looking up, the sky was pure powder blue.

It wouldn't have made a difference even if it had been a blizzard. It wouldn't have dampened my spirits. Nothing could, not even the uncomfortable rub of the soggy elastic of my comfy supermarket knickers against my pregnant belly, because I had a man who loved me, a baby on the way and, thanks to hard work, determination and a bit of sheer luck, my debts were all paid off. It seemed that finally, I may have got my life sussed.

CHAPTER 2

"I'm nervous about telling everyone," I admitted, as I pushed open the wooden gate leading into my parents' garden. "My friends must have their suspicions because I've not been drinking at Christmas parties, but my mum and dad are going to be shocked."

"We did a pretty good job of keeping it to ourselves though, didn't we?" Max chuckled. "I didn't think we'd manage to hold it in this long."

"Nor me."

The temptation to share our news had almost got the better of me many times since the positive test. After all the times I'd heard my brother talk of how much Noah, Alicia and Imogen meant to him I wanted to let him know I understood, really understood, in a way only someone who had already fallen totally in love with their unborn child could, how much of a miracle and a blessing it was.

"They're going to be happy for you, Soph. Happy for both of us." He suddenly looked worried. "Unless you know something I don't. They don't hate me, do they? Think I'm not good enough for you?"

"Don't be ridiculous," I guffawed, "they love you, you're already one of the family. That's not why I'm nervous about telling them. I just don't want them to know that we, you know…" My voice trailed off and I raised my eyebrows twice in quick succession to get my point across.

"They know we share a bed. It's not that much of a leap for them to take a guess at what we do when we're there. They've got three kids of their own, so they obviously know all about the birds and the bees."

"Don't." I clamped my hands over my ears to block out the horrific imagery running through my head. Cheers, Max. "Thinking about my parents' sex life makes me feel queasy, and I'm only just getting over the morning sickness."

"Come on," he said, knocking on the front door before turning the handle and walking into the hallway of my childhood home. "They're going to be over the moon. A new grandchild to spoil and love, and their firstborn becoming a mummy. That's a celebration waiting to happen."

I knew he was right, but it still felt a bit like, by walking into the kitchen and getting out the scan pictures, we might as well shout "WE'RE HAVING SEX!" at the top of our voices. I had to get over it though, because despite no visible bump my trousers were already getting tight. I thought lustily about the maternity jeans I'd seen in Mothercare's window just the week before. Then I'd been giggling at the swath of navy fabric designed to cover and support a mother's bump, but even just one week on that excess material – super-soft excess material at that – seemed inviting and necessary as my jeans and still-damp pants rubbed harshly against the skin of my stomach.

I didn't have chance to dwell on my thoughts of comfy clothes though, as my mum poked her head around the kitchen door, her cheeks smudged with flour where she'd wiped her hands against them as she baked. She couldn't help herself – whenever she knows I'm coming over she makes my favourite rich chocolate cake, topped with Smarties, just the way she'd made it as a treat when I was a child.

"Sophie!" she exclaimed, as though I hadn't told her we'd be coming over at teatime and me and Max turning up was a complete surprise.

"Hi, Mum."

I stretched my arms around her neck and enveloped her in a hug. She smelt the same as she had when I was a little girl, vanilla-sweet, and as she planted a kiss on my cheek – something I'd normally pull away from – I couldn't help but think that I was soon going to be a mum myself, and how I never, ever wanted to kiss my child and for him or her to pull away. I wanted to smother them with kisses, shower them with love, and for me to be a comfort to them.

Everything my parents had done for me flashed before my eyes.

All the nappy changes and sleepless nights – I was a notoriously bad sleeper as a baby, apparently. Dad can't believe they had two more children after me and risked even more nights of broken sleep.

The school runs and the loads of washing.

Taking me to majorettes, and piano lessons, and ballet classes.

The sleepless nights (again) when I was an unruly teenager, using the house like a hotel and my dad as a taxi service at some ungodly hour.

There had been times I was sure I was failing them, disappointing them, but our home and their hearts had been filled with nothing but love.

I'd become so wrapped up in my thoughts that I'd not let go

of Mum, and if it weren't for one of her wiry chestnut curls tickling the skin on my neck I'd have gladly stayed in her embrace for longer.

"Are you all right, pet?" Two lines of concern appeared between her eyebrows as she looked me up and down. "You're not sick, are you? I've spent all afternoon baking your favourite chocolate cake. You can always take it home for another day, I suppose."

"I'm not sick, Mum. Why would you think that? Do I look pale or something?"

"No more than you usually do," she said, but there was suspicion in her tone. "I still can't get used to you not being orange," she teased. "When you used to go for those spray tans it was like having an Oompa Loompa coming to visit."

Max laughed. He didn't know me when I was high maintenance, but he'd seen the photos, and even I had to admit I looked like a different person. Not worse – at least, I didn't think so, and neither did Max if the way he couldn't keep his hands off me was anything to go by. I still took my time over my make-up most days, but didn't lay it on as thick as I used to. The honey-blonde highlights I'd once sworn by were a thing of the past too, although my hair was naturally fair anyway, so it didn't look radically different. All the pampering I'd insisted was a necessity had finally been seen for what it was – a luxury, an expense I could do without. I'd been amazed by how much I'd previously been spending on beauty treatments.

"I don't know why you're laughing, Max Oakley," I jokingly chided. "I know you've been using my tinted body lotion. That bottle's going down way quicker than it usually does."

"I'm not getting involved in your little domestic," Mum said with a chuckle, heading back into the kitchen. "This cake needs to come out now before it catches around the edges."

Max grinned, then leant down and whispered into my ear.

"Although you would have been my favourite Oompa Loompa by a mile."

"I wasn't orange!"

"You were a bit," he said, almost apologetically. "Look."

He handed me a silver frame from next to the landline phone and I studied the photo, taken at Nick and Chantel's wedding. The blushing bride, swamped by her meringue-style princess dress, and my younger brother looking rather dashing in a classic film-star kind of way, in traditional top hat and tails, smiled back at me. My dad was in the same get-up as my brother, although at six foot three already, the top hat made him look even more pencil-thin than usual, and my mum beamed beneath a wide-brimmed hat that matched her cerise and white floral dress. My sister, Anna, the middle sibling, had her arm looped through Dad's and I stood on her other side.

From the colour of my skin you'd think I was just back from a fortnight in the Maldives, but my tan was one hundred per cent salon and zero per cent sunshine. The wedding had taken place in January, and everyone knows winters on Tyneside are harsh. As well as the time spent topping up my (fake) tan, I'd been dedicatedly moisturising my lips to ensure they didn't get chapped; I'd wanted to ensure they were a smooth base for the latte-coloured lip-gloss I'd favoured back then.

"That feels like a lifetime ago. A lot has changed since that day."

I placed the photo back where it lived, nestled amongst pictures of my nephew, Noah, from his recent nursery photoshoot, without mentioning my ex-boyfriend Darius, who'd been my plus one for Nick's wedding. It had been him who'd taken the family photo.

"For the better, I hope?" He smiled. "And there are going to be plenty more changes to come over the next few months."

"I can't wait," I said, taking his hand in mine as we moved into the living room. "Things are about to get exciting."

CHAPTER 3

*D*ad was in his usual seat at the left-hand side of the sofa, dozing as the TV talked to itself. It was one of those "Escape to the Sun" shows about moving to the continent. Every so often Mum threatens to up sticks and start afresh, and since she and Dad retired they'd spoken about it more and more, but they're Newcastle through and through. Visiting my sister and her partner in Austria twice a year is as close as they were likely to get to moving abroad.

"Hi, Dad," I said, raising my voice to a shout in the hope of stirring him. When he didn't move a muscle I knew I'd have to go in hard if I was going to drag him out of his slumber. Honestly, it'd be easier to raise the dead.

I sank into the vacant seat on the settee and moved nearer, until my lips were close to his ears, grey hairs poking out wildly.

"BOOOO!" I shouted, right down his lughole, at the same time as I jabbed him in the ribs with my finger.

"Whaaaa?" he shouted, sitting upright and looking around the room in confusion. "What is it?"

A giggle escaped my lips. He looked like he belonged in a

sitcom, with what was left of his hair sticking out at all angles, and his wide-eyed daze at being startled.

"You'd fallen asleep on the settee. Again."

I wrapped my arm around him affectionately. I've always been a daddy's girl, as has Anna, and there's not much better than his hugs.

"Oh, Sophie! Max! I'd forgotten you were coming over tonight. I wasn't sleeping though, I was just resting my eyes."

"Yeah, right." I laughed. He always said that. "Had a busy day?"

"Pretty hectic, actually. You think retirement is all lazing around, but it's not. This morning we were at the supermarket, then popped to the sorting office to collect a parcel, but ended up stuck in a queue for half an hour. Every time I see one of those red slips the postman leaves, I groan. Then we met Finley and Joel for lunch at The Bull – they send their love, by the way, and told me to tell you they're buying a cockapoo – and when we got back here I put my feet up for five minutes and now you two are here."

"Nothing wrong with a daytime nap, Mr Drew," Max said.

"How many times, call me Bob. Mr Drew makes me feel like an old man."

"You are an old man," I teased. "Look at that hair, grey and receding."

"The cheek of her," Dad said to Max, with a cock of his head. "I happen to think it makes me look distinguished. Grey hair's in fashion these days. Look at how mad the ladies go over George Clooney. It's not done him any harm."

"Did someone mention George Clooney?" Mum piped up. "I've always had a thing for him." She turned to me. "I've been watching the repeats of *ER*. Even though I've seen it hundreds of times it's worth watching again. That man's a real silver fox."

"See?" Dad replied triumphantly. "Grey hair's for sex symbols these days, not just grandads from Newcastle."

Max and I shared a look, and he nodded his encouragement to prompt me.

"Funny you should say that," I started, reaching into my handbag for the little card containing the scan picture, "because we have some news."

Mum gasped as what I was hinting at hit home, her hand flying to her face to cover her gawping mouth. Dad, bless him, didn't seem to have a clue what was going on.

"Really?" she said finally. "You're having a baby?"

"We are," I confirmed, beaming at Max. "It was the scan today, that's why we've not been at work, because we've been at the hospital."

"And everything's all right with you and the baby?" Mum's voice wavered, and I knew she was sharing the same concerns I'd had myself. After what our family had been through it would have been weirder if we hadn't been cautious.

"Everything's wonderful," Max assured her. "Everything's perfect."

Mum's eyes were damp as she studied the photo, delicately but deliberately tracing our baby's outline with her finger.

"Hello, little one," she whispered, and the tears that had been clinging to her eyelashes loosened their hold and flowed freely down her face. "I'm your nana."

My dad still hadn't said a word, only just coming round from his dreamlike state.

"Congratulations, Pumpkin," Mum said, as she wrapped one arm around me and the other around Max in a move that wasn't far off being classified as a headlock. "Congratulations to you both. What lovely news for a Wednesday afternoon. I can't believe it, can you, Bob? Our Sophie's going to be a mummy!"

When Mum finally stopped squeezing us, I turned to face

Dad, afraid his silence was masking his disapproval. It had happened fairly quickly after all, and although neither of my parents were particularly old fashioned, Max and I had only known each other for less than a year.

A jolt ran through me as I saw he too was tearful.

"Are you okay, Dad?"

He used the back of his hand to wipe away a tear as he nodded.

"I always worried about you, Soph. You'll know what it's like yourself, when your little one arrives. All a parent wants is for their children to be happy, and you never seemed sure what it was that would make you happy."

"I'm happy, Dad," I assured him, "really and truly. Max and this baby are all I need. It feels like everything's falling into place in my life, at long last. I've never felt so content."

"That's all I want to hear," he said. "Now, do I get to see this picture of my beautiful grandchild?"

Mum, her face still stained with tear-tracks, handed him the picture, and I suddenly saw my dad differently, his vulnerability right there on the surface rather than buried the way it usually was. When I was a child I'd always thought he was brave and strong, the way all girls think their dads are, but as he took in the image there was a fragility.

"Beautiful," he said, his voice breaking. "Congratulations to the pair of you."

"This calls for a celebratory treat, don't you think?" Mum wafted her hands in front of her eyes to stem the tears. "And I know just the thing."

Max smiled. "Chocolate cake?"

"Chocolate cake," she confirmed. "It's always been my baby girl's favourite."

And then I started crying too, hormone-fuelled tears of joy, because all I ever wanted was right in front of me.

CHAPTER 4

"You're kidding? You're pregnant?"

Tawna looked at me in disbelief. Anyone would think I'd told her we were expecting a flamingo, not a baby.

"Yeah." I smiled. "Me and Max are expecting a baby. Due at the end of spring. We had the scan in the week, and it's been killing me not telling you two, but I wanted to tell you in person. Some things are too big to share on WhatsApp."

My cheeks were flushing red; I could feel the blood rushing to my head. I'd thought sharing the good news would get easier, but it still felt strange, as though I was bragging about a swinging-from-the-chandeliers love life and super-fertile eggs flowing from my ovaries.

"That's fantastic news." Eve pulled me in for a hug. "You're going to be brilliant parents, I know it."

"Congratulations," Tawna said, joining the hug. "I can't believe you're having a baby!"

People must've wondered what was going on, the three of us blocking the doorway to Jojo Maman Bebe in an emotional huddle, so we composed ourselves before going into the shop and oohing and aahing over the cute miniature clothes hanging from racks in colour order – pastel pink, powder blue and perfect unspoilt white.

"Look at this," said Eve, one hand over her heart and another holding the world's tiniest coat hanger aloft to brandish a red-and-white striped Babygro. "You've got to get this, it matches your top."

She pointed to my T-shirt, a trusty Breton-striped design that I'd keep in my wardrobe until it fell apart, because the nautical look comes around again and again. Each year I thought the spring/summer fashions would alter, but stripes were timeless and classic, even though they did get a bit wibbly when stretched over my large (and soon to be getting larger) boobs. The Babygro was a scaled-down replica, although my T-shirt didn't have a pair of press-studs at the bottom to hold a nappy in place (although after the pressure on my bladder at the scan I could have done with the reassurance of a nappy. The relief when I'd finally been allowed to go for a wee was like nothing else).

"It is cute," I admitted, fingering the brushed-cotton fabric. "Although is it too much to be matchy-matchy with a baby if you're not a celebrity? I don't want to be a laughing stock."

"Your baby, your rules," Eve insisted. "It's no one else's business how you dress them."

"Except for Max," I pointed out, although I couldn't see him having an issue with an inoffensive Babygro.

"Except for Max," she agreed, although Tawna, who was admiring a hooded cardigan complete with bear ears, shook her head fervently.

"I disagree," she said. "Max is a decent guy, and he loves the bones of you, anyone can see that. But his sense of style..." Her nose wrinkled in disapproval.

"What's wrong with his style?" I asked defensively. "I like the way he dresses. Smart casual. We can't all have partners who wear Savile Row suits on a daily basis," I joked, referring to Tawna's husband, Johnny, a successful local businessman who rocked the formal "hottie in a suit" look.

"I never said there was anything wrong with the way Max dresses, there's no need to be so sensitive. If you'd let me finish, what I was going to say was that his sense of style isn't as defined as yours. This baby's going to have good genes, you want to make the best of it by dressing it well."

"Clothes are clothes," Eve shrugged, "especially for a baby. I don't think many newborns are stressing over whether their threads are on trend."

The comment didn't surprise me – Eve had never been as bothered about fashion as Tawna and me, and although she dressed well, she wore styles she knew suited her slender figure rather than whatever items were hailed as the latest must-haves by the glossy magazines.

"I totally get what you're saying, and I agree, up to a point. But my parents have photos of me dressed in some disastrous outfits as a toddler, and I don't want to subject this little one to any horrors."

I rubbed my stomach, small concentric circles massaging my belly.

"That's why you need to take charge of baby's wardrobe," Tawna said pointedly. "It's never too young to be stylish."

Eve rolled her eyes skywards but remained silent.

"Maybe you're right. Perhaps I will buy this after all," I said, reaching out for the red-and-white striped Babygro. "Baby's first outfit."

I smiled, a fizz of excitement exploding in my stomach at the milestone.

"You know it makes sense." Tawna grinned.

As I handed the item to the cashier to put through the till, I picked up a catalogue from the counter, thinking how easy it could be to revert back to my old ways of overspending. The world of baby accessories was both tempting and pricey. Maybe next time I hit the shops I'd do it without Tawna in tow. Shopping with my two besties was like having an angel on one shoulder and a devil on the other. No prizes for guessing which friend had a halo and which was encouraging me to spend...

CHAPTER 5

We stopped to rest at a café, one we always went to when in town because of their amazing chocolate éclairs, pumped full of cream that can't help oozing out of the pinholes it's been piped through. The decadent layer of glossy dark chocolate was, quite literally, the icing on the cake. We had one each – even Tawna, who had given up on the faddy dieting she'd been prone to since getting married. I allowed myself to eye up the triple choc muffins piled high behind the glass of the counter, using the excuse I was eating for two when I bought one to take away.

"Anything else you need to buy?" asked Tawna, examining the bottle of nail polish she'd bought earlier. She shook the bottle, tapping the glass against the heel of her hand, before unscrewing the lid and painting a thin layer of the sparkly taupe polish over her nail. The heady smell turned my stomach.

"I need to get a piece of red felt. I'm making Christmas stockings for the nieces and nephews."

"I meant for the baby!"

"Oh." I laughed. "Well, I wanted a pair of maternity jeans,

but they're so expensive. Maybe I'll see if I can find some second-hand ones." I sighed.

Second-hand clothes weren't the issue. Since tightening my belt charity shopping had become one of my favourite hobbies, a way to feed my retail therapy addiction without losing complete control of my finances (and with Max managing a charity shop I had my pick of the items that came in). It was more that the skin on my stomach was pressing harder against my jeans with every bite of the éclair, and although my stomach was more choux pastry than baby, I wasn't under any illusions. It wouldn't be long until nothing in my wardrobe fitted.

"Clothes are a necessity," Tawna encouraged. "Maybe you could try a pair on? We have to go past Mothercare anyway to get back to the Metro."

"People will look at me and wonder what I'm doing. I'm not even showing yet."

My curvy figure meant that although I was quickly heading towards the halfway point I didn't look pregnant, more just like I'd had a larger-than-normal Sunday roast, with double helpings of crumble and custard.

"You're not showing, but you're still pregnant, and you have to be comfortable," Eve said rationally. "I'm with Tawna on this one, you're going to have to wear something."

"Maybe I will try some on," I said, easily influenced. "If I find a pair I like I might be able to get the same ones cheaper online."

"There are baby fayres too, aren't there? I've seen them advertised on Facebook. People sell their maternity clothes and baby stuff because it's practically unused. I bet if you look online you'll find some locally."

Eve was straight on it, tapping away at her phone screen to find an event in our area.

"Look, there's one next weekend at the leisure centre. You

should go, Soph. I bet you'd be able to snap up loads of bargains from your list."

She referred to the shopping list on the back of the magazine I'd picked up. "Essentials" they'd called it, although I'd never even heard of half the stuff on it. Muslins? A steriliser? And would I really need a breast pump? It sounded more like an instrument of torture than a childcare necessity.

"Would it be tempting fate?" My stomach churned again, and I couldn't tell if it was down to the potent fumes from the nail polish or out-and-out fear. "People get superstitious about buying things too early, don't they?"

"Be positive," Eve said, reaching out to rub my shoulder reassuringly. "If anything was going to go wrong – which it absolutely isn't, by the way – it would have nothing to do with whether or not you've bought a bouncy chair or a mobile to hang over the cot."

"I know, I know. And I do want to be organised. I'm just nervous."

"I think that comes with being a parent." Eve smiled. "You've got a lifetime of worrying about this baby ahead of you."

"Thanks." I laughed, before sarcastically adding, "That's really reassuring."

Eve poked her tongue out in retort. "You know what I mean. Anyway, it's up to you. If you want company, I'm free next weekend and happy to tag along, and if you don't I'm sure there will be another one before you pop."

"Urgh, I hate that term." Tawna pinched the handle of the brush of the nail varnish between her fingers, careful not to smudge her newly painted nails. "It sounds like something from a horror film. I don't want to think of Sophie popping, thank you very much."

"Have you seen *One Born Every Minute*?" asked Eve. "Giving birth is beautiful and natural. The female body is amazing. Did you know the vagina stretches to four or five times its usual size during birth? I think having a baby must be pretty empowering, actually."

Talking about stretchy vaginas wasn't enough to put Eve off her éclair. She took a generous bite.

"Can I get over the queasiness and the tender breasts before we start analysing the birth?" I said lightly, although I was only half joking. I wanted to be as blissfully ignorant about that part of the process for as long as possible. "I know it's got to come out one way or another, but I don't want to spend the next five months panicking about it. I hate it when women play birth top trumps, scaring pregnant women with their own experiences of epidurals that didn't work and massive forceps being shoved up their foof. Marcie told me about her stitches in great detail yesterday. I've never clenched my legs so tightly in my life. Now that's a horror story."

"Ignore her. Your body will do what it was designed to do, and the NHS will look after you if you do need some help."

"It's a shame my mum's retired," said Tawna. "She'd have loved to deliver your baby."

I'd forgotten Mrs Maguire had been a midwife, and a highly thought of one at that. I remember going to Tawna's bowling party for her thirteenth birthday and a woman coming up to her and hugging her. It had transpired that Tawna's mum had delivered the toddler twins strapped into the wide double-buggy she was pushing and the woman was grateful for her assistance in ensuring she'd had the birth experience she'd wanted. I'm not sure Mrs Maguire's no-nonsense approach was what I needed though. I'd always found her intimidating.

"The midwife who did my booking visit was lovely," I said. "Really calming, even when she was jabbing me with a needle for the blood tests. She reminded me of your mum, Eve."

Eve's mum, who'd pretty much been a second mum to me too, had recently been diagnosed with early onset dementia. The diagnosis had been upsetting for Eve, who'd never known her mum to be anything other than competent and strong, but there had been an element of relief too as it had explained the change in her behaviour. What had started out as small laughable errors, things like putting liquid soap from the dispenser that sat on the sink on her toothbrush instead of toothpaste, or accidentally using orange juice instead of milk in her morning coffee, had escalated until her lack of awareness of danger was a risk to herself and others.

"She's doing really well. She still likes the care home and the staff there are brilliant. They have all sorts going on. When I visited last night she was playing bingo and there's someone who goes in to run an armchair exercises class. I was worried she'd feel patronised by being treated like an invalid, but you know how sociable she is. She's revelling in it."

"That's good," Tawna says. "And is she happier about you selling the house now?"

Eve was moving out of the family home in the hope it would encourage her mum to sell it, which, in turn, would help fund her care.

Eve shook her head. "Mum's come around to the idea that we need to sell it, and there's no point in it sitting there empty once I move, but she's still not happy about it. I've got to admit I've found it weird seeing the For Sale sign outside too. It's weird to think I'll be in a flat of my own soon."

"It'll be good though, having a place of your own."

"And it'll cut down on the work commute. Less time stuck in traffic jams being closer to the city centre."

"Speaking of which, any news on Dudley retiring yet?" I said with a wink. Eve had been waiting for her line manager to leave for years, ready to swoop in and claim his role as her own. He'd recently turned sixty-five, so Eve was sure an announcement would be coming sooner rather than later.

"Funny you should ask..." Eve said in a teasing tone, but the enormous grin on her face told me and Tawna all we needed to know.

"No way!"

"Seriously? He's finally hanging up his lab coat?"

"Yep." Eve grinned, her eyes sparking with excitement. "Decided that since his wife's already retired he might as well do the same so they can enjoy life. They've already booked a Norwegian cruise. He's always wanted to go and see the Northern Lights. Which frees up the position of lab manager for someone else."

"That's great news, Eve. I know how much it would mean to you to get this promotion."

"It's not in the bag yet though," Eve warned me. "I'll still have to go through the interview process and it'll be advertised externally as well as within the company. I'm sure I'll have stiff competition."

"No one would be a match for you," Tawna said generously, even though neither of us really knew exactly what Eve did at work. Her degree was in chemistry, and her PhD was something related to that. Once when I met her from work she'd still been wearing plastic safety goggles like a nutty science professor, having forgotten to take them off. She'd tried explaining what she did before, but it went straight over my head, the science lingo being way beyond my GCSE level knowledge.

"She's right," I said loyally. "You'd be an asset to them, and they know how dedicated you are. I don't know anyone who puts in more hours than you do, except maybe Tawna's Johnny. If they don't give you the job, I'll be banging on their door demanding to know why."

"The advert's going out next week, so I'm going to be busy

working on my application." Eve pulled a worried face, although I could tell she was excited deep down. This was what she'd been waiting for, after all. "I just hope I'll get an interview. I'm better at selling myself face to face than I am on paper."

"They'd have to be nuts not to give you an interview," Tawna said.

"I agree." I raised my hand to second the motion. "You'll walk it. They know how good you are at what you do, and that if they don't offer you the role you'll have to look for something elsewhere. They'd be crazy to give it to anyone else."

"I hope you're right," Eve said, before polishing off the last of her éclair with one more orgasmic groan. How she made it last that long I don't know, mine having disappeared in three seconds flat. "So, are we hitting the shops again or heading home?"

"I would like to try on those jeans." I slid my hand between my stomach and the fabric of my jeans to stop the denim chaffing against me. "Even if I don't buy them today, it'll give me an idea. Maybe I can find out what muslin squares are too while we're there."

"Sounds good to me." Tawna knocked back the last of her cappuccino.

"Sounds good to me too." Eve tapped her hands against her thighs as though that'd push her into action.

"To Mothercare!" I announced, sliding my arms into my jacket.

"To Mothercare," my friends echoed in unison.

JANUARY

*W*ithin ten days of our scan, Max and I had told everyone who needed to know our happy announcement. Christmas celebrations had given us the perfect opportunity to spread the news. Family, close friends and work colleagues shared in our excitement.

The only person who'd seemed distant was Chantel, which had surprised me. She was the most maternal person I knew, an absolutely devoted mum to Noah and the twins. I expected her to be cock-a-hoop about becoming an auntie for the first time. Instead, her smile hadn't made it as far as her eyes, giving her a strange look of a ventriloquist's dummy. When I'd mentioned it to Max he'd suggested that perhaps my sister-in-law was jealous, because our baby would mean Alicia and Imogen would no longer be the youngest in the family. Either way, her lukewarm reaction had left a smear across the memory of sharing our news with my brother, Nick.

However, despite Chantel's diffidence and my own deep-rooted panic that things could still go wrong, I was determined to enjoy my pregnancy.

I was, however, a bit overwhelmed by how much baby stuff

there was at the baby fayre. It was the equivalent of a car boot sale, with individual pitches from sellers with their goods laid out on blankets on the floor or on a tabletop. Baby bouncers, slings, high chairs, and a ridiculous amount of plastic baby baths were on display and although I'd come armed with a list, I still didn't know how many items on it were really "can't live without them" necessities and how many were optional extras pitched as must-haves by manufacturers to easily swayed newbie parents.

"It's so busy," Eve exclaimed in disbelief. "I didn't realise these events were so popular."

"It's because it's run by the NCT. I've been reading about them on the pregnancy forums online."

"Is that some kind of club for pregnant women?" asked Eve. "I'm sure someone at work went to antenatal classes run by them."

"That's right." I nodded, keen to impart my new-found wisdom. "They run classes to help prepare for both the birth and parenthood. It's not just for mums though, it's for dads and birthing partners too. We've already contacted them to let them know we're interested in classes because there's a really high demand."

Max had been the one to give me the details of the local branch after his sister-in-law, Belinda, had eulogised about how much information she'd gained from her group during pregnancy.

"She said the couples they met have become some of their best friends," he'd enthused, although I'd inwardly groaned at the thought of forcing friendships with people just because they happened to have had unprotected sex at a similar time to us. I had friends already, I didn't need any more.

"I suppose everyone wants to be as well informed as they can be about it all," Eve said, pressing a button on a toy. She jumped back in surprise and horror as a clown with a creepy smile sprung up out of the box, bobbing from side to side in a sinister manner, before squashing his body back down and clamping the lid shut tight.

"You know I've always wanted a family, but it's only since I started reading anything I could about pregnancy that I realised how little I knew about the whole process."

"Science never was your strong point," Eve teased, and I knew she was thinking of the time I managed to singe my chemistry homework (which had been copied almost word for word from Eve's anyway) on a Bunsen burner. "Although, I thought you'd know about the birds and the bees at your age."

"The birds and the bees, yes, but the growth of a foetus, no. It's been a revelation learning all about what's happening inside me. And the strangest thing is knowing there's a little person inside me and not being able to feel him or her moving. I can't wait to feel it move."

"You won't be saying that when you're a week overdue and baby's bouncing on your bladder," a woman with a beach ball bump interrupted. "I can't remember the last time I had a decent nights' sleep."

"Preparation for when they're out," said the woman behind the stall. She was pushing a buggy back and forth to try to get her toddler to sleep as she talked. "This one thinks 3am is party time. He's wide awake and ready for the day, even though it's pitch-black outside."

She tried and failed to stifle a yawn. "I'm shattered all the time these days."

"Worth it though, I bet," Eve said, smiling at the sight of the curly-haired cherub fighting sleep.

"Well worth it," she said, her eyes twinkling through their bleariness.

Seeing her love, so visible, obvious and unconditional as she stared at her child, gave me a rush of excitement about meeting my baby, and my hand automatically moved to my stomach to massage the first hint of bumpage. It was something I'd seen expectant mothers do so many times, and being honest I wondered if they were doing it for attention, as though to remind the whole world there's a little person growing inside them. Now it was happening to me I realised that wasn't the case at all. It was instinct, a longing to connect with and protect the person I'd not yet met but who I already loved with all my heart and soul.

"How much are you asking for this?" I pointed to a zebra print bouncy chair. I didn't buy into the whole "pink for girls and blue for boys" ideology, but, being a fan of colour and pattern, found myself naturally drawn to what people class as gender-neutral. The fabrics I used when crafting were almost always bright and colourful repeating patterns or bold floral designs. The zebra print was right up my street.

The lady named her price, not breaking her repetitive rocking to answer, and I nodded in acceptance. She was asking far less than the cost of similar items I'd seen in catalogues and online. Sure, there was a part of me that would love to be able to splurge on all new items and for everything in the nursery (actually a box room, but it would be a nursery when Max and I finally got around to shifting all the crap we didn't ever use out of it) and where everything matched like a magazine spread, but it wasn't worth getting into debt over. As long as Baby was warm and safe. They wouldn't be getting stressed about the lack of colour co-ordination.

"First purchase of the day in the bag," Eve said, taking the bouncer straight out of my hands.

"I love it," I admitted. "But you don't have to carry it, I can manage."

"You're pregnant." She looked at me as though I was a bit dim and might have forgotten.

"That's right, I'm pregnant. I've not woken up to find my arms have suddenly disappeared." I chuckled.

"If I carry it, it'll be easier for you to look at the stalls," Eve reasoned, and as I spied a table piled high with maternity clothes I was grateful for her help. "Honestly, it's not a problem."

"Thanks. You're the best."

"I know," she joked, before shooing me in the direction of the clothes I'd been eyeing up. "Now go and see if you can grab any more bargains. You can't live in that one pair of jeans for the rest of your pregnancy."

I didn't need telling again, and before long I was rifling through the clothes. Some of them were pretty awful – shapeless tent dresses in dull sludge-like shades of brown – but there were a couple of pairs of jeans which I kept hold of, and a cute summery red-and-white polka dot dress which I liked, even though I worried I'd end up looking like a pregnant Minnie Mouse in it.

I held up a top covered in multi-coloured stars of all sizes, trying to figure out why it had a lining. My confusion must've been evident on my face as the woman selling the clothes helpfully explained it was a breastfeeding top.

"You lift one section up and bring the other one down," she said, demonstrating on another top with the same cut. "It means you can whip your boobs out to feed without feeling like an exhibitionist. With my first one I was petrified of anyone seeing my nipples, because I couldn't separate the sexual side of them from the practical mummy side. By the time I had my third I was getting them out anywhere and everywhere, not caring who saw." She laughed, poking her finger through the gap she'd created between the layers of material and waggling it about. It looked surprisingly like a freshly tweaked nipple, perky and erect.

Everyone was so open. Was that what happened when you had a baby, you overshared with people you'd only just met? I couldn't imagine being this frank with strangers, and I wasn't a prude. I spent most of my early twenties gyrating against men I didn't know in sweaty nightclubs wearing nothing more than glitzy boob tubes and skirts that barely covered my arse. Hardly the behaviour of a shrinking violet.

"I hadn't given breastfeeding much thought," I lied, trying and failing to drag my eyes away from the lady's waggling finger.

"Oh, you must breastfeed!" the woman exclaimed. The horror that I might do anything else was obvious from her gaping mouth and startled eyes. "It's best for Baby and helps build that special bond between mother and child. Helps with losing the baby weight too, and I needed all the help I could get on that front. I put on five stone when I was pregnant with Milo. Five stone! Soon pinged back into shape though with the help of Mother Nature," she said proudly.

I wasn't really interested in the woman's vital statistics, nor her strong opinions on the benefits of breastfeeding. Whether or not I'd take that route would be a decision made further down the line and based on more than one woman's opinion.

I did want the maternity jeans though, so I thrust them at her with the sweetest smile I could muster and asked her how much she wanted for them. One pair, the darker of the two, looked barely worn, and the other pair, more distressed in style, were still in good worn condition. The price she suggested sounded fair – roughly half the cost of buying the one new pair I'd had my eye on in town – so I gladly took them off her hands and scuttled back to Eve to escape any more pearls of mummy wisdom.

"I didn't realise people were so..." I floundered for the word,

"...so... defensive over how they choose to parent."

Eve frowned. "What do you mean?"

"Everyone's so keen to point out how they dealt with labour pains, and what they did to get their child to sleep through the night as though it'll work for everyone else," I huffed. "They think their way is the right way."

"Maybe they're just trying to help?" Eve suggested kindly (and naively).

"Nuh-huh," I said, with a shake of my head. "It's almost like they're showing off, a 'look how well I'm doing' kind of thing."

"They're not all like that, Soph," Eve said with a disapproving tone. "Sure, there are a few who want to share their opinion..."

"More like ram it down my throat," I interrupted, my comment earning a disapproving glance from my friend. "They're all really opinionated."

"Not all of them, actually. I was talking to a lovely lady over there." Eve pointed in the direction of the fair-haired woman standing behind a table covered in blue and green clothes. "She's got a toddler already and she's pregnant with her second."

"You wouldn't think she'd want to sell everything if she's having another," I pondered, taking a closer look at the lady. She had a neat and tidy bump which looked as though it had been stuck onto her frame, along with that radiant glow that pregnant women are supposed to have. I'd always thought it was mythical, but no – she definitely had it.

"She's just been told she's having a girl," Eve explained. "She's keeping a lot of the neutral stuff to reuse, but said her mum-in-law refuses to let her dress a little girl in denim dungarees with a fire engine emblazoned on the bib. She's trying to make some money to buy some dresses and girly things to get her off her back. Some of the stuff she's selling is brand new with tags!"

That grabbed my attention. Something about finding a pre-owned yet unworn item excited me, especially when it came to baby clothes.

"Shall we go and look?" I said, trying to sound casual. "You know that even though pink's my favourite colour I don't believe in the whole 'clothes for boys and clothes for girls' bullshit."

Eve shifted the bouncy chair from under one arm to the other.

"Come on then," she smiled, "I'll introduce you to Iris. But don't spend too much money! You've got plenty of time to get everything you need."

I knew she was right, and I didn't want to spend unnecessarily but the thrill of the shop raced through me. And what was it Tawna had said? Everybody needs clothes.

As we got closer to the table, I could tell I wasn't going to leave empty-handed. Although the clothes would definitely be marketed as being for boys – the table was full of khaki greens and navy blues (and some disgusting sludgy-browns that I can only think were chosen for their ability to disguise leaky nappy mishaps) that designers favoured for boys while girls got delicate lemons and pastel pinks – I loved the prints on some of the Babygros. Bold and bright fire engines, smiley tabby cats and sparkly robots adorned the miniature outfits, and Eve was right – some were brand new with tags, in front of a handmade sign stating "everything £1".

"She'd be able to get much more for these on eBay," I whispered from behind my hand. "I'd feel bad buying them for this price."

That's when I spotted the sweetest pair of dungarees I'd ever seen – powder-blue corduroy with dark blue accent stitching. I couldn't stop myself from reaching out and fondling the material, the furry texture tickling my skin.

"Hi," the lady said warmly, smiling at Eve. "Is this the friend you were telling me about?"

Eve nodded. "Iris, meet Sophie. Sophie, Iris."

"Nice to meet you," I said, taking in the woman in front of me.

Her honey-blonde hair was scraped off her face into a messy bun (a proper messy bun, not one of the strategically styled ones the celebrities have for the BAFTAs or the Emmys) which drew attention to the crop of freckles peppering her nose. She looked to be totally make-up free, either that or she'd mastered the au naturel look, but her skin was flawlessly smooth. She dressed as though she was going to the gym – flared black yoga pants that clung to her bump and a white vest top, although a splodge of orange, which I suspected was regurgitated carrot, decorated her shoulder. It was the splodge that made me warm to her. It made her appear human, unlike some of the robo-mums.

"Eve was telling me you've just had your first scan. How're you feeling? Over the morning sickness?" Her voice was cheery and light, with an Aussie twang.

"It's been more nausea than morning sickness," I said honestly and, even to my ears it sounded apologetic. "There were a couple of days right at the start where my stomach would churn at the smell of bleach in cleaning fluids, and I was really tired before I even knew I was expecting, but other than that I've been really lucky."

"Sounds like how I was with Jude." She nodded to the curly-haired boy asleep in his buggy. "I was sick once, although I still think that was because I chain-ate a multi-pack of Mars bars rather than morning sickness. But with this one..." she fondly stroked her bump, "...the first trimester was a nightmare. It got to the stage where I'd bring Jude's toys into the bathroom so he could amuse himself while I had my head down the dunny. I was being sick all the time. Then as soon as I hit thirteen weeks I felt fine again. It was weird."

"I'm twenty weeks," I said, my voice wavering. "Hopefully I'm not going to start feeling crap now."

"I'm sure you won't. You'll be in the blooming stage. Although sounds like you've had that all the way through." Iris laughed, before saying, "If you see anything you like, feel free to make an offer. I just want rid of all this," she added, sweeping her hand across the "stock" as though sprinkling it with magic dust. "My wife's sick of the amount of boxes of baby clothes and she's said two's her limit, and as this one's a girl I'm going to go all out on pink and flowery clothes."

"These are gorgeous. I love the designs."

"My mother-in-law runs a baby boutique so she got all this at reduced rates. With Jude being her first grandchild she got overexcited and gave us way too much, and because he was a whopper of a baby he never even got to wear half of it. It's a shame really, but that's why I want it all to go to a good home."

"So will your mother-in-law supply you with just as much in the way of dresses?" I asked.

Iris nodded. "She was as excited as I was about the thought of another girl in the family. It's different for me, because I'm one of three girls, but Jessie – that's my wife – she's an only child, and even all her cousins are male and none of them have got kids yet either. This baby is going to be so spoiled."

"I know it's not very PC to say it, but it must be nice to know you'll have one of each," said Eve, and for a moment I wondered if she was feeling broody. She'd always been so academic, so career focused, and because she'd been single for such a long time neither Tawna nor I had ever seriously considered Eve's credentials for being a mother. Thinking about it she'd be brilliant. Funny, kind and able to do whatever homework was set, even rock-hard algebraic equations.

"I was over the moon when we were told this one was a girl," Iris admitted, her voice low. Anyone would think she was admitting to a cold-blooded killing spree from the shameful way she said it. "Don't get me wrong, I'd have been delighted with another boy, but I love Jude so much that I already feel as though I'm betraying him by having another. At least with a girl it takes out that one element of competition."

"I can see that." I picked up the dungarees, along with a selection of Babygros, their thick off-white price tags dangling. "I'll take these, please. Although it feels like daylight robbery only giving you a pound each for them. You've got so much lovely stuff here."

"I've told you, you're doing me a favour." Iris grinned, taking the note I offered her as payment and stuffing it in the margarine tub that was doubling as a makeshift till. "Listen, I know this might sound weird, but would you like to go for coffee sometime? There's a group of us who get together with our toddlers."

"That would be lovely," I said, my heart warming at the thought of having made a new friend. Perhaps I wasn't so against the notion after all. "I'll give you my number if you like?"

"Write it down here," Iris said, handing me a flyer and a biro. "I'll text you the details. They're a decent bunch," she added as I scribbled down the numbers.

"I'll look forward to it."

It would be nice to get to know Iris better. Tawna and Eve were great friends but with the best will in the world they couldn't understand what I was going through. How could they? They'd never been pregnant themselves. Maybe this was the start of me forming part of a mummy clique of my own.

As Eve and I said goodbye to Iris, our arms weighed down by my haul, a bubble of anticipation fizzed in my chest. I knew when I got in Eve's car the first thing I'd be doing was checking my phone, to see if Iris had already messaged me.

As I walked up the short path to the door of our mid-terraced house, awkwardly juggling my purchases, I was struck by the sudden urge to go to the loo. When I'd been speaking to Iris, sharing my good fortune when it came to morning sickness and other pregnancy-related ailments I'd forgotten how my bladder was constantly screaming at me these days. Back when I was a party animal I'd get a similar sensation towards the end of a night out – when I'd had a skinful of alcohol and made the mistake of taking that first fatal pee which opened the, erm... floodgates. There was a genuine risk that if I didn't make it through the door and to the toilet, I'd wet myself.

I used my elbow to ring the doorbell, knowing that by the time I located my keys which would no doubt be hidden in the bottom of my handbag beneath a load of receipts and empty chocolate bar wrappers (don't judge, babies need sustenance) it'd be too late. Max was definitely at home – his car was parked on the road outside and I could see the flicker of the TV screen through the living room window – so with any luck he'd let me in.

I was jiggling on the spot as he answered the door wearing a bemused expression. I must've looked like a walking jumble sale with the carrier bags stuffed full of goodies, the bouncy chair and a plastic baby bath someone foisted on me saying, "Take it, I'm only going to bin it otherwise," and as I pushed past him, unceremoniously dropping everything to the hallway floor and running to the bathroom, he called up the stairs after me.

"Have fun? Looks like you and Eve bought a few things?"

I pulled at the waistband of my maternity jeans and sank onto the pine loo seat, sighing with relief at having made it in time.

"It was hit and miss," I called, "but I managed to get some bargains. It was nice to be able to buy a few bits and pieces, actually. I know it's still early, but I couldn't help myself."

"A parcel arrived when you were out," he called back, and although I was probably imagining it I was sure I picked up a hint of judgement in his tone.

"I've not ordered anything."

I wracked my brains in case I'd forgotten, but I was sure I'd not bought anything online. Gone were the days of having online spending sprees in the hope it would cheer me up. The rush that came with buying the item had always been followed by a rapid wave of fear when my bank statement arrived, showing how each purchase had pushed me deeper and deeper into debt.

"Are you sure? Maybe you ordered something when you went shopping last week and forgot about it?" I could hear the doubt in his voice. "It's a pretty big package..."

"I think I'd remember if I'd ordered something," I snapped.

"I was only asking. It's an exciting time, and I know you'll be looking forward to buying everything the baby needs."

"And I am, but the only things I've bought are one little outfit and the things I got at the sale today."

"Then why's there a Moses basket in our hallway?" Max

must have believed me, because his voice sounded genuinely puzzled rather than laden with judgement.

I tore off a strip of toilet paper and wiped, dropped it in the bowl, flushing the chain and washing my hands, before stepping out onto the landing. The parcel caught my eye and the fact I'd failed to notice it on the way up proved how desperate for the loo I must have been. When Max said "pretty big", he wasn't joking. It was enormous, and there was a large cardboard box propped against the wall too. When I looked more closely I could see the black lines of an image illustrating a rocking base for the basket.

"When was this delivered?" I spluttered, the cogs of my mind manically whirring.

"About half an hour after you left. I just assumed you'd seen something you liked and gone ahead and bought it."

"Big purchases should be joint decisions. I wouldn't have gone out and bought something like this without talking to you about it. This is your baby too."

"Then where's it come from?" Max sighed with frustration, his eyebrows furrowing so low that they hid behind the upper rim of his glasses. "Could your parents have ordered it? Got a bit over excited at the thought of a new grandchild?"

I shook my head.

Mum and Dad weren't the sort for flamboyant gestures and over-the-top gifts, and although they'd offered to buy us something to celebrate our good news I knew they meant further down the line.

"I could ask *my* parents if they ordered it, I suppose," he said slowly, although that seemed equally as unlikely as my parents unexpectedly splashing out.

"They'd have told you if they were going to buy something. And they'd have asked our opinion on it first, not just gone charging in like a bull in a china shop and bought it."

"You're right. Dad would have mentioned it when I spoke to him yesterday."

I leant over to check the delivery slip, wondering if it might reveal where the packages had come from. It crossed my mind that perhaps it wasn't meant for us, that maybe it should have been delivered to our neighbours instead (although one side was occupied by an elderly couple and the other two students; a Moses basket and stand didn't really seem a likely purchase for either).

"You'd think it'd have details of the account it's been bought from," I said, scrutinising the sheet of paper for clues. "There's nothing on here at all – no customer name, no email address, not even the price."

"Let me see," Max demanded, taking the pale green slip from my hand. When his eyes had scanned the print, he jabbed his finger against the paper. "Look here. It says it's a gift."

"And it's definitely meant for us?"

"It's addressed to you."

He handed me back the paper and I looked at the address at the top. Our house number, our street. And at the top, in block capitals, my full name, SOPHIE ELIZA DREW. I'd never been a fan of my middle name, which was why it wasn't on any of my bank cards or school certificates. Other than legal documents where they had to be stated – namely my birth certificate and my passport – it was easy to avoid. The fact it was there, on top of the statement of purchase in black and white, made me wonder if maybe the delivery was my parents' doing after all. However much I grumbled about my name, my mum always harped on about how much she loved it, inspired as she was by Eliza Doolittle (the one in *My Fair Lady*, not the one-hit wonder noughties popstar).

"I'll ring my parents," I said, wondering how to approach the conversation. "Perhaps it was them after all."

I headed into the lounge, sinking into the Ikea sofa I'd bought after seeing it advertised in a newsagent's window, and called my parents, even though deep down I didn't believe it had been them.

When Mum denied all knowledge I knew she was telling the truth, and Dad, bless him, wouldn't even think of making such a huge gesture without her to prompt him. She was definitely the one with the get up and go in their relationship.

When I hung up and ended the call I was no clearer about where the parcel had come from. Max's parents had also feigned ignorance, and although there were lots of friends and family members who'd shared in our excitement when we'd told them the news, I couldn't think of any who'd make such an extravagant gesture without telling us first, and hardly anyone knew my middle name.

Picking up the delivery sheet I looked at the shop it had been delivered from, a megastore specialising in items for babies and children. Nick and Chantel had bought lots of stuff from there when they'd been expecting Noah, and I knew it wasn't cheap, but with my sister-in-law still acting strangely whenever I rang it seemed unlikely they'd be behind the Moses basket.

Maybe it was my work colleagues chipping in and buying a big gift? They'd been so thrilled when I'd told them the news, all of them loving Max now they knew him (especially Kath, who'd jokingly told me that if I got to the point where I'd had enough of him to pass him on to her. At least, I hope she'd been joking. When it comes to Kath and sex I'm never quite sure). I'd have to ask them if the surprise delivery was their doing on Monday. It had to be them, I thought, as I made my way to the toilet for what felt like the millionth time that day. It had to be. Who else could it be?

CHAPTER 8

"How're you doing today, Sophie?" Jane was stood, as usual, in the kitchen waiting for the kettle to boil. She was a world-class procrastinator, but also really good at her job, which was just as well. Marcie wouldn't stand for anyone taking the piss.

"Yeah, I'm fine," I said, trying to find a way to broach the subject of the mystery Moses basket. If it was from the women at work I didn't want them to think I was ungrateful.

I'd even phoned my sister to see if it was her doing – it hadn't seemed likely but, to give Anna her dues, she had been making more of an effort lately. I had my suspicions Mum might have told her how I'd previously felt left out because of the closeness of my siblings' relationship.

"What did you get up to at the weekend?" Jane enquired. "Weren't you at that baby sale?" she asked with a chuckle.

I gave her a questioning look. "What's funny about that?"

"I always find the posters for those funny. 'Baby sale'." She giggled, waving her arm dramatically in front of her like a used car salesman showing off the vehicles on his forecourt. "It

45

sounds like they're selling the babies," she explained, when I shook my head in confusion.

"Ah." I smiled, although my mind was still mulling over how I was going to ask the difficult question. Maybe Jane wasn't the right person to ask, with her flights of fancy and her own strange train of thought. "I get it now."

"Did you buy anything?" she asked eagerly. "They're meant to be good, aren't they? When I had our Sean, my sister gave me everything she'd used for my nephew so we didn't have to buy a thing. It was great, of course, but it would have been nice to have chosen some things ourselves. She even gave us the nappies! Of course, it was different in those days. I still used terry towelling ones. Now it's all disposables."

"People do use reusable nappies, but they've had an update," I said, explaining all I'd learnt from the internet about wraps and liners. "We'll definitely try them. The amount of disposables that end up in landfill each year... it doesn't bear thinking about." I shuddered.

"It's no good for the environment," Jane agreed, as the kettle came to the boil. The steam puffing out of the spout left a layer of condensation on the beige tiles that covered the walls. "I understand why people use them though. The washing and drying is a lot of work, or it was in my day. I swear the smell of Milton sterilising fluid still turns my stomach. The bathroom reeked of it for years from the nappy bucket. Disposables are convenient, and everyone has busy lives these days."

"I won't be working though, because I'll be on maternity leave. I'm sure I'll manage," I said cheerfully.

Jane gave me a dubious look as she drowned a teabag and lumped in three heaped teaspoons of sugar before giving the drink a stir.

"Did you want a hot drink?" she asked, and I shook my head.

"I'm trying to have more water," I replied, pulling a face as I reached for a glass from the cupboard on the wall. "All I want is a decent cup of coffee, but I'm cutting back to one cup a day. I'm not just thinking about myself now. This little one might not be in the mood for a shot of caffeine," I said, rubbing my hand across my stomach.

"You could try decaf?"

The look I shot back was enough for Jane to know I disapproved of her suggestion. What's the point in decaf coffee? The buzz was the main appeal.

I turned on the cold tap, thinking about the unexpected delivery as I caught the water in the scratched-up pint glass and decided I might as well be brave and broach the subject. After all, if it was my work mates who'd sent it, then the mystery would be solved and I was all up for that to happen. Although Max had said he'd believed me when I'd denied making the order, I got the distinct sense that he didn't fully accept that I had nothing to do with the Moses basket. When I'd pointed out that although the delicate white broderie anglaise was pretty it wasn't my style, he'd seemed placated, but it wasn't nice feeling that my partner – the father of my baby, for crying out loud – didn't trust me.

"Jane?" I started, before taking a gulp of water. The cold tasteless liquid trickled down my throat without any of the caresses my usual morning coffee would have given me. "This is probably going to sound really weird but did you, Marcie and Kath send me something over the weekend?"

The bewildered look on Jane's face told me all I needed to know. Admittedly, she never looked particularly alert, but it was obvious she didn't have a clue what I was talking about.

"I don't know about Kath and Marcie, but I've not sent you anything," she said. "What would I send? It's not your birthday yet, it's one of the few I know without having to check my calendar with it being on Valentine's Day."

"Oh, it's nothing," I said, downplaying the uncomfortable feeling creeping over me. "A parcel arrived and we didn't know who it was from. I thought it might have been you lot clubbing together to surprise me."

"No, it wasn't us." She scooped the teabag out of the mug and flung it into the bin. Drops of tea splattered against the white of the bin liner. "Perhaps it was one of your friends doing a good deed?" she suggested.

I'd already thought of that, and mentioned it to Tawna and Johnny, Eve, Joel and Finley... even my substitute grandma, Norma. Her and Fred, her late husband, had always liked to spoil me. Usually it would be with a Dairy Milk or a bag of liquorice – something small – but Norma had been so delighted at our news that I thought it was a possibility that she'd splashed out with a big present. They'd all denied it.

"I'm running out of people who I think it could be from," I said, "and it was addressed to me, not Max, so I don't think it can be from anyone he knows."

"Could you ring the shop? They might be able to tell you who bought it."

I shook my head. "Already tried that. They said they weren't able to pass on any details because of client confidentiality. It's annoying."

"You can see their point though. They can't go giving out their customers' details willy-nilly."

"I don't get it. Why would someone send me a present and not put their name on it? It doesn't make sense."

"I'm sure whoever did it just forgot. I've done the same thing myself when ordering gifts online; Sean wondered where the nose clippers I'd sent him for his birthday had come from. It'll be an error."

I nodded my agreement, and echoed that she was probably right, but couldn't shake the uncomfortable feeling.

I was glad when she changed the subject, asking if I had any plans for after work. For once I had something more interesting to report than going home to craft in front of the telly.

"I do have something planned for tonight," I said, trying but failing to hide the enormous smile that had crept onto my face. "A woman at the baby sale invited me to meet up with her and her friends and they're getting together tonight so I'm going along. They usually meet for brunch but tonight they're having a dinner party."

"Lovely." Jane smiled back. "I made some fantastic friends when I was pregnant, some of them are my closest friends to this day. You can't underestimate how important it is to find people going through the same thing as you. Pregnancy can be a funny experience, especially if none of your old friends are going through it at the same time."

"Iris, that's the woman I met, is pregnant, but I'm not sure if any of the others will be. They know each other from when they were pregnant before – Iris has already got an eight-month-old."

"Maybe you'll be able to glean some pearls of wisdom from their experience," Jane said, before taking a sip from her tea. "I hope you get on with them all anyway."

"Me too," I replied. "Me too."

CHAPTER 9

I'd been distracted from my work all day, thoughts of how the night was going to pan out running through my head. Would the mums like me? Or would they think I was imposing on their tightly-formed friendship group? I'd only met Iris so far, and although she'd been lovely and down to earth, would the rest of the gang be as open to a newbie joining their fold?

When I'd phoned Max to explain my worries, he'd tried his best to put my mind at ease. "You'll be fine, Soph," he'd said with his usual warm lilt. "Iris wouldn't have invited you if she didn't think you'd fit in."

"It's a bit weird though, isn't it? Making new friends at our age."

I couldn't remember the last time I'd made a new friend. Tawna and Eve had been part of my life for so long that I couldn't remember a time without them, and my other mates, such as Joel and Finley, had been around almost as long. The women at work were probably my newest friends, or Nadia, Darius's ex who, after a rocky start where I'd convinced myself she'd had it in for me, had turned into someone I had a laugh with over social media, but she lived in Liverpool so I didn't get to see her often.

"Our lives are going to change beyond all recognition. It's not going to be long before we'll have antenatal classes and we'll meet other people in the same situation there. Then it'll be playgroups and Tumble Tots, then the parents at the school gates. Over the next few years we're probably going to meet more new people than we have over the last decade just because we'll be thrown together. Everyone says the same, their friendship circle changes and grows when they have kids. It's part of the way life changes."

"But what if they don't like me?" I said, vocalising the fear that was working its way into my psyche. "We're meeting at Iris's house. It won't be easy to make excuses and leave."

"Sophie, they're going to love you. Be your usual kind, funny self and they'll be putty in your hands."

"You're sure?"

"I'm sure. I've got to go, the area supervisor's coming to the shop this afternoon and I want to make sure it looks as good as it can. But stop worrying!"

I tried, I really did try. But my stomach was still churning every time I thought about walking into a room full of people who were already close, scared of the possibility of rejection.

❧

"Sophie! I'm so glad you came!" Iris bundled me up in a hug which wiped away some of my nerves. Not all of them though, because I was well aware that all eyes were on the stranger (in other words, me).

"Thanks for inviting me." I looked around the room.

It was homely and warm, with magnolia walls, a fluffy cream carpet and dark grey settees. The settees were practical for family life, the walls and carpet less so. Surely with such light colours they were asking to be splattered with paint or for play dough to be smooshed into the ply? Framed pictures of Iris and a woman who I assumed must be Jessie were propped up on the mantelpiece, along with a number of photos of Jude, and a plant pot containing a bright poinsettia sat on the windowsill. But I wasn't taking much notice of the décor, even though I usually loved nosing around other people's houses. I was too self-aware.

"This is Rachel," Iris added, pointing out a slender lady with wild red curls that looked like corkscrews. "And I can see Mia's here now." Iris waved at the chocolate-brunette through the window. "She didn't think she'd make it until later, because her husband, Giles, doesn't finish work until seven," she explained. "He must have made it home early."

"Hi!" Mia waltzed in, full of joie de vivre. With her pillar-box red lipstick and swooshes of dark eyeliner she looked like she'd stepped straight off the cover of a magazine. "I'm Mia, you must be Sophie."

She leant in to give me a continental kiss – on both cheeks, but without connecting.

"Hi," I said, as she leaned back, raising my hand in an awkward, embarrassed wave. "I'm Sophie. But you already know that."

"Iris told us our group was expanding," said Rachel with a smile. Her accent was pure BBC English, her teeth large and horsey. It crossed my mind that she might be aristocracy. There was something about her that reminded me of a minor royal. "Lovely to meet you, Sophie. Iris said you're pregnant with your first?"

"That's right," I replied, instinctively placing my hand on my stomach. "Due in May."

"You timed it well. Better than sweating like mad in a crazy heatwave." She laughed, a pretty, tinkly laugh like a child's. "If I have another baby I'm going to aim to get pregnant in the summer so by the time I'm showing I'll be glad of the extra insulation."

Rachel's warmth made me feel instantly welcome, as did Jessie and her home-made flapjack. Even Mia's overfamiliar air-kisses helped me feel like part of the group, and it helped that the women were funny and friendly, and obviously shared my love of baked goods if the way they clamoured for Jessie's oaty bake was anything to go by.

"We didn't plan it this way..." I started, before correcting myself. "We didn't plan it at all, actually. Let's just say that this baby came as a big surprise to both me and Max."

"It's worked out well for you then," Mia said, her eyes – almond in both shape and colour – sparkling. "We were trying for two years before we hit the jackpot, and it nearly killed our relationship. You'd think all that sex would mean we were closer than ever, but it caused no end of arguments. I was so desperate to be a mum and Giles was adamant he wouldn't go and see a doctor. He couldn't bear to think there was a problem with his little swimmers."

I blushed at the personal nature of the conversation, wondering how Giles would feel to know his sperm were being discussed at length with a total stranger. I know Max would hate it if he thought I was discussing the intimate details of our private life with all and sundry.

"But it all worked out in the end," I said, hoping that would put a stop to the conversation, and the image of tadpole-like sperm that had made its way to the forefront of my mind. "Do you have a boy or a girl?"

"A boy," Mia said, her face lighting up. "Byron. He's just starting to pull himself up on the furniture and it's like parenting has shifted to a whole new stage."

"That's what happens," Rachel said with a wise shake of the

head. "You just get to grips with one part of the parenting process and then something else comes along which throws you completely."

"Rachel's a gap parent," Iris explained. "Her eldest is away at university, her youngest is the same age as Jude and Byron."

I was stunned that Rachel was old enough to have a university-aged child. I thought she was slightly older than me, but not much. Cripes, it wouldn't be physiologically possible for me to have a child of eighteen, being the late bloomer that I was. I'd willed my first period to arrive for the first three years of high school, and when the first deep-red blood stained my supermarket knickers soon after my fourteenth birthday I'd been so happy I'd cried. Both Eve and Tawna had started years before and my lack of menstruation made me feel like an outcast. The novelty had soon worn off though when I'd realised the inconvenience and having to remind Mum I needed tampons and painkillers added to the big shop. My periods had continued to be an irritant right up until discovering I was pregnant – irregular and heavy – as far as I was concerned the lack of bleeding was a bonus side effect of pregnancy.

"Rach is brave starting over again," Mia agreed. "Once I get back to having a full night's sleep I'll be reluctant to give it up again. That's why me and Giles are trying again now, and hoping it won't take as long to get caught this time around."

"A big age gap wasn't in my plans either." Rachel took a sip of wine. She tilted her head back and closed her eyes, savouring the taste. Weirdly, I didn't fancy it at all. "I was only sixteen and it was quite the scandal at the time. I was away at an all-girls boarding school and my boyfriend went to the boys' school in the same town. I went home for the summer and Mummy knew something was up before I did. She made me take a pregnancy test and it was positive. She and Daddy tried to encourage me to have an abortion, but I couldn't go through with it, so I dropped out of school. When Verity arrived I didn't have a clue what I was doing – I'd never even held a baby before – but I was determined to be a good mum to her, even if I was only young."

"What did Verity's dad say when you told him?" I asked, curious. I knew I was prying, but all these women were so candid that it didn't feel like I was asking for more than they were willing to share.

"Timothy was horrified," Rachel said with a grimace that made me feel bad for mentioning it. "He said it was up to me to do whatever I thought was right, and that he'd support me either way, but he was very clear that his plans weren't changing. He had his heart set on going to university and becoming an architect, you see. And you've got to remember that my parents lived in Kent, nearly two hundred miles from where we were at school."

"So what happened to Timothy? Does he see his daughter?" I asked, and everyone around me dissolved into laughter. "What?" I asked, puzzled at their response.

"He's my husband," Rachel said, holding up her left hand to show off a solitaire diamond ring and a plain gold wedding band. "We always knew we were meant to be together, but we were way too young when we had Verity. We needed to see a bit of life first. We got back together five years ago, and then Xander arrived last year. Parenthood's certainly been a different experience for both of us this time around."

"I'll bet. That's such a lovely story though." The romantic in me was swooning like a good 'un at the thought of all they'd been through together. "It shows that true love always finds a way."

"So what about you?" Rachel asked. "Have you got someone sweeping you off your feet or are you doing it alone?"

The thought of having to cope with a newborn without a support system made my blood run cold – I'd be useless. I couldn't even keep a houseplant alive, so the chances of managing to keep a real-life human being, however small, safe from harm didn't fill me with confidence. Thankfully Max was as caring as they came.

"Me and my boyfriend have just moved in together," I began. "Well, he's moved in with me, I suppose. He's really excited about being a dad even though it happened far sooner than we'd planned. He's been reading all the pregnancy books and telling me what's happening with the baby's development each week."

"Aww, how sweet," said Iris. "He sounds like a keeper."

"I think he is." I smiled. "I can't imagine my life without him."

"If that's not a sign that you two were made to be together, then I don't know what is," said Mia.

"I'm really lucky."

"I think we all are," said Mia. "A supportive partner makes all the difference when your hormones are on the rampage."

"Absolutely," said Iris. "Jessie must be an absolute saint to put up with me. I'm so demanding, and I know it. I made her go out to the all-night garage at midnight last night to fetch me a carton of orange juice because I was craving it."

"But I bet she did it without complaint," Rachel said. "That's what love does."

"I complained," Jessie said with a laugh, "but only because I was already in my PJs. I'd do anything for this one." She reached over and gave Iris's arm an affectionate rub.

As we carried on talking about love, life and pregnancy, I was glad I'd been brave enough to come. These new friendships felt like ones that would be worth nurturing.

CHAPTER 10

"How did it go with your new besties?" Tawna asked drily, the following Friday night.

Tawna had invited Eve and me over for a barbeque and had shown a real interest in how the gathering at Iris's house had gone. At first I'd thought she was jealous of me branching out – although Tawna has always been popular, she isn't always the best around new people because she has a tendency to be full-on – but her sly comment made me wonder if actually she was jealous that I wasn't hanging around with her.

"It was great," I replied, ignoring the tone of my friend's original question. "They were really nice. Iris and Jessie, they're the couple whose house I went to, are around our age, and Rachel's a bit older – and a bit posh, actually, she even went to boarding school – but she was nice. Then there's a younger woman called Mia, and honestly, she's stunningly gorgeous. She's got a curvy figure and these gorgeous eyes that seem to change colour in the light, and she's got this amazing haircut, a bob with a harsh fringe. She's like a cover girl."

"Sounds like you've got a girl crush," Eve teased, and I could feel my cheeks hotting up.

"Don't be ridiculous," I scoffed. "All I was saying is she's captivating to look at. I'm a bit intimidated by her, if I'm being honest."

"But she wasn't bitchy to you or anything?" Eve asked. "Sometimes beautiful people are so used to getting their own way that they don't have any manners."

She didn't mention my ex, Darius, but I thought that was yet another not-so-subtle dig at how, despite his good looks, he was only out for what he could get for himself. Thank goodness I was now immune to him. In the past he'd turn on his charm and I'd be putty in his hands.

"It's not 'Mean Girls' for mums, it was just a get together. She was really nice, they all were," I said protectively. "It's just strange to make a whole new group of friends at our age."

"It'll be good for you," Eve said encouragingly. "Us two will always be here for you, but neither of us have had a baby. We can't tell you whether what you're going through is part and parcel of being pregnant or if it's something you need to get checked out, so for what it's worth I think it's great that you're reaching out and meeting new people."

Tawna still looked like she'd been sucking on something sour, but she said, "Eve's right. It'll do you good to be around people who understand what you're going through."

There was an uncomfortable tension in the air, although I wasn't quite sure why. Changing the subject seemed a good option, so I quizzed Eve. "Any interest in the house yet?"

"Two young families came to look at it on Wednesday night and one of them was really keen."

"That sounds promising," I said, holding tightly crossed fingers aloft. I knew how much of a difference it would make to both Eve and her mum if the house could be sold – Mrs McAndrew's care was necessary but expensive. "I guess the estate agent will chase it up?"

"They're coming for a second viewing on Sunday. I really hope this is it," Eve said, "because being a homeowner is an expensive business and I know once I move into the flat it'll be a case of continually throwing money at it in one way or another – insurance, decorating – and that's without even mentioning the mortgage itself. It's endless."

"Your mum's house will sell soon, and it'll be easier then," Tawna assured her. "Things will fall into place, I know they will."

"I hope you're right," said Eve, scooping a large dollop of mayonnaise onto her salad. "Life's chaotic enough with work and visiting Mum, and what with going for the promotion and trying to sell the house on top of it, I'm slowly losing my mind."

"You're not," I assured her, reaching out and rubbing her shoulder. "You're doing great."

"Sophie's right," Tawna added. "There's no way you're losing your mind. You lost that ages ago."

Eve gave Tawna some serious side-eye, but the corners of her lips were curling up into a smile. "Very funny. So, what's new with you, Mrs Hamilton?"

"Only the usual. Nothing exciting."

"No holidays booked?" Eve asked, and when Tawna shook her head we both tried and failed to hide our surprise. Holidays were a big part of Johnny and Tawna's life – Johnny worked incredibly hard and had always been of the mindset that to counteract that he should play hard too, with multiple holidays each year to exotic climes, but looking back their last big holiday had been their honeymoon to Cuba. They'd had a couple of weekend trips away in this country, one to a cottage in the Cotswolds and another to St Andrews for Johnny's university reunion, but there hadn't been the usual regular extravagant holidays.

"We're going to Norfolk for a week for our anniversary,"

Tawna said, fondling the pendant on her necklace. "We've booked a gorgeous stone cottage within walking distance of the beach."

"Sounds romantic," I said with a smile. "Lots of hand-holding and moonlight strolls along the sand?" I teased.

"Maybe," Tawna replied, "or maybe we'll spend the evenings watching the sun go down from the garden. It's got gorgeous views." She pulled out her phone to show us the photos, and I had to admit the cottage looked gorgeous and cosy, and the views across the coast were spectacular. "Either way, it'll be good to escape from here for a while. Shame it's ages away."

The comment set off a flicker of concern inside me but, knowing Tawna's reluctance to ever admit that life was anything other than perfect and in her control, I let it go. She knew where I was if she needed someone to talk to.

But although Eve and I stayed at her house for five hours, Tawna didn't mention anything that would raise alarm again, instead being the perfect hostess as she ensured we were well-fed, always had a drink (fruit juice for me) and had a backing track of our favourite songs to keep us upbeat.

FEBRUARY

CHAPTER 11

For the whole drive to the hospital Max and I continued the discussions we'd had about finding out the gender. It had been a real debate, with me desperate to know and Max wanting to wait until the birth.

The second scan had come around quickly, having not found out we were expecting until so late on.

"You could go out of the room and they could tell me in private?" I suggested, to which Max had looked horrified. "Or we could ask them to write the sex down on a piece of paper and put it in an envelope, in case you change your mind and want to know?" I asked hopefully, thinking I could steam it open when Max was out. He often got home from work later than I did, so I'd have plenty of opportunity.

"I won't change my mind." His tone was gentle but firm. "What's the rush in knowing? It doesn't make any difference to me whether we have a son or a daughter and we'll buy neutral clothes."

I kept my lips buttoned tightly, but after seeing Alicia and Imogen dressed head to toe in pale pink – soft corduroy pinafores with floral tops underneath – I'd swayed towards the idea of the traditional gender colours, especially if we had a girl. Pink had always been my favourite colour, ever since I'd been given a Firefly My Little Pony for my sixth birthday. It had been a present from Eve, actually, and was probably still boxed up with my other childhood toys in my parents' loft.

"It'd be nice to know though, wouldn't it?" I persisted. "It'd make it easier when choosing names."

Max had been spending his evenings poring over the baby names book Nick and Chantel had passed on to us, folding down the pages of any names he liked. Some of his choices were suspect, but he was taking it seriously.

"It'll be a boy," he said, as though that was the only option. "I'm one of four boys, my dad's one of two boys, my grandad was one of six, all boys. Grant and Chris's children are boys. It's in the Oakley genes."

"Do you really think so?"

I wasn't unhappy at the thought of a boy – if anything I loved the idea of a mummy's boy to dote on me and gross me out with jokes about poo and willies. But there was a tinge of sadness too at the things I would miss out on; wedding dress shopping with my daughter and crying like a baby at the first glimpse of her head to toe in white.

Snap out of it, Sophie, I told myself. This child hasn't even been born yet and already you're marrying them off. And boy or girl, all that matters is that they're happy and healthy.

"We'll find out, won't we?" he said, and I jolted with joy, thinking he'd come around to my way of thinking about finding out the sex. He must have detected my excitement as he added, "When Baby arrives."

My shoulders sank.

"It's not that long to wait. It's your birthday next week, then it'll be Easter. May will be here before we know it."

May felt like a very long way away to me. A very long way away indeed.

The snot-like jelly was cold on my stomach once more, and although I should have been prepared for it, I wasn't. I don't think Baby was either, because a weird sensation took over my stomach, almost like a bubble popping within me.

"I'm sure I just felt the baby move." I laid still in anticipation of a repeat performance, but nothing happened. "Maybe I imagined it," I added quietly, as Max and the sonographer watched, waiting.

"Have you been getting much movement?" the sonographer asked. "Usually by this stage you'll be feeling a few wriggles."

"Nothing yet." I sighed. I'd been desperate for the reassurance feeling Baby move would bring, even though Rachel had said it was a bit like having an alien inside you that you had no control over. "I'd thought I'd be able to feel something by now."

"It might be the position Baby's in, meaning you're not feeling the movements. Once there's less room in there the kicks are more obvious."

"I guess I'll just have to be patient," I said with a smile, but the disappointment was obvious in my tone.

"Let's take a look," the sonographer said, pressing the probe firmly against the now-slippery surface of the taut skin of my stomach. My shape had changed considerably over the past week. Although I'd never classed myself as thin, nor even curvy due to the soft folds of skin around my middle, whereas before I'd looked podgier (part of the reason I hadn't realised I was pregnant until I was so far along – I'd put the weight gain down to contentment and Max's knack of rustling up all manner of culinary delights in the kitchen of an evening), I now very definitely looked pregnant. Not because my bump was huge – it wasn't by any means, but where I was carrying the weight was different, the swell starting immediately beneath my boobs whereas before it was all around my stomach and bum.

"There we go," the sonographer mumbled to herself. "One baby."

She moved the wand around, varying the amount of pressure she applied, before tilting the screen so Max and I could get a view of what was going on inside my body. Seeing baby head-banging in my stomach when I couldn't feel a thing was bizarre to say the least, and a laugh escaped my lips.

"Baby looks to be having a good time in there." The sonographer smiled. "I need to take a few measurements to make sure everything is as it should be. I'll be as quick as I can, but it sometimes takes a while so just relax."

I couldn't peel my eyes away from the screen, my heart full of love for the little person writhing around within me. I tried to decipher whether they looked more like me or Max, even though the picture wasn't especially clear and in all honesty it was most likely too early to be able to tell. I was in awe of the arms and legs moving away like an uncoordinated raver, and wondering if we were going to have a dancer on our hands when I felt the sensation again, as though my stomach was rotating. It wasn't unpleasant as much as it was unfamiliar.

"I can feel it again," I whispered, turning to face Max. "It's a really strange feeling."

"Probably Baby telling me to stop poking," joked the lady, although she didn't stop probing and click-clacking on the computer as she took the measurements.

"Now," she said finally, "do you want to know the sex? Because if you don't, I'll turn the screen away from you. Sometimes these babies like to flash their parents."

I looked pleadingly at Max, turning on the doe-eyes.

"There's no need to turn the screen," Max said, and I let out a squeak of excitement. "We want to know if we're having a son or a daughter."

As he squeezed my hand, the love pulsing from his body to mine, Baby moved again, a more definite movement, as though aware of how momentous the occasion was, or maybe I was beginning to recognise that the swirling sensations inside me really were my future son or daughter's movements.

"Right then," she said, prodding even more determinedly, "let's take a good look."

Baby wriggled, a flash of bottom mooning at us on the screen, and I caught my breath as the sonographer angled the probe to get a better view and enable us to discover the sex of our child.

"You're having a girl," she said finally, before removing the probe. "Congratulations!"

"A girl," Max echoed, a faraway look on his face. "We're going to have a daughter."

I couldn't reply, scared that if I so much as tried I might burst into tears. Instead I nodded, my heart swelling with love for Max and our little girl. Our daughter.

CHAPTER 12

"Who are we going to tell first, your parents or mine?" I asked, secretly hoping we'd be able to go to my mum and dad's. It wasn't that I didn't want Hector and Andrea to know, and I knew they'd be thrilled about the first female addition to the family in a very long time, but this was something I wanted to share with my family as quickly as possible. After so long feeling like I was on the fringes of my family, worrying that my lack of vision and ambition was a let-down, I couldn't wait to share our news. It felt like this baby was my greatest achievement, the one time I was following convention.

"We can tell your parents first, if you like," Max said amiably, and my heart gushed with love. I knew he must feel the same about wanting to tell his family. Even though he got on perfectly well with my mum and dad, the Oakleys were so tight-knit that he must have been bursting to give them the vital update. "Do you want to go now?"

I looked at my watch, the winter sunlight catching on the glass of the face. Three o'clock. Since Dad took early retirement he was home most of the time anyway, but Mum flitted in and out of the house with her job as a make-up rep. Afternoons tended to be quieter though, with her waiting until the workers got in from their heavy days at the office before collecting their orders and dropping off deliveries.

"And you're sure you don't mind?" I said, remembering how my parents had also been the first point of call when we'd had the initial scan.

"Whatever makes you happy."

And that was why I loved him so much, because he genuinely did value my happiness above his own.

"Let's go to my parents on the way home," I said with a smile, placing my hand in his. "And then we'll go to your parents too. They'll all be wanting to know how we've got on."

I could feel the pops in my stomach as we made our way to the car, like a million tiny bubbles bursting at my core. I had Max by my side and our daughter happily tucked up in my womb. It was the best feeling in the world.

"A girl? Are you sure?" Hector Oakley looked mildly bemused by our announcement, his heavy brow furrowing in confusion. "Us Oakleys don't do girls."

"We do this time," Max affirmed. "They showed us the images and it was most definitely a girl. Sophie and I are having a daughter. You're going to have a granddaughter."

Andrea's eyes were brimming with tears, and she clutched her hand to her chest, her trembling lips pressed tightly together to stop the tears from falling. "A little girl. What brilliant, brilliant news."

She stepped forward and threw her arms around first Max and then me, her grip so tight it was almost suffocating.

"And everything is as it should be?"

"Everything is perfect."

"Andrea's going to spoil this baby so much," Hector said. His voice was gruff but teasing. "The first girl in our family. She won't know what to do with herself."

"I don't have the experience of girls, do I?" she said, patting my arm gently. "But I will now. You know we'll be here for you and helping out whenever we can. If you want a night out we can babysit, you just need to say the word."

"Give them a chance." Hector laughed. "Let our granddaughter make her appearance into the world first."

"Thanks, Mum, we'll remember that," said Max, although I couldn't imagine leaving my baby with anyone, not even Max's mum. It wasn't anything personal against her – she was obviously a very maternal woman and had done a great job with all four of her sons – but I wasn't ready to think about being apart from my child just yet.

"I bet your parents were over the moon too, weren't they?"

"They were ecstatic." I laughed, joy washing over me at the happiness on my mum's face as I'd shared the news. "Mum was in tears before I'd even told her, and as soon as I mentioned it was a girl she was a mess."

"It must be emotional," Andrea agreed. "It's one thing finding out your son's going to be a father, but quite another to know your daughter is becoming a mother. Knowing they're carrying a baby and have the birth to go through must be both exciting and nerve-wracking all at once."

"What were your births like?" I asked tentatively, because although I'd made fun of the openness of the women from the antenatal groups for their out-and-out oversharing, I had become mildly obsessed with hearing about other women's birth stories, even the horrific ones. It was as though to be forewarned was to be forearmed, knowledge holding power.

"Grant was big – 9lb 6oz – and it felt as though my labour

was going to last forever. When my waters broke I was in denial, because I hadn't thought about the birth. I had to call Hector home from work to drive me to the hospital and he asked me if I could hold the baby in until his shift finished." She threw her husband a dismissive roll of the eyes. "When I got to the hospital I was exhausted and they had to use forceps to help him out, which was the scariest part – I didn't even know what forceps looked like until the doctor was holding them up, and the thought of them being put into my nether regions..."

The look on both Max and Hector's faces were pictures, and I wished I had my phone to hand to capture their horrified faces.

"Anyway," she continued, "it was worth it in the end, and he was perfect. Big, but perfect."

"What about Max?" I asked.

"He was the other extreme. Where Grant took ages, Max practically shot out, it was like shelling peas. I'd only just got out of the car and onto the ward when he arrived. He was the easiest of the lot. Chris was breech, see, so I ended up having a planned caesarean, and the same happened with Dale. It was hard trying to recover from the stitches when I had four boys all demanding my attention."

"You were brilliant," Hector said, admiration obvious in his eyes. "As you always are. I knew you were strong, but I never realised how strong until I saw you as a mother. It wasn't just the births, it was how you were afterwards – gentle and loving and patient, but solid with it. No nonsense."

"Didn't have much choice." Andrea laughed. "They'd have run rings around me if I'd let them. Not that they didn't all have their moments, this one included," she said, ruffling up Max's hair. He shook his mum's hand away and brushed his fingers through his hair, but the affection was obvious. They had a strong bond that I only hoped I would have with our daughter.

"Tell me more." I loved hearing about the parts of Max's life

I'd missed out on, the thirty years that had passed before our paths had crossed.

"Oh, nothing that terrible," she said with a flick of the hand. "The usual teenage high-jinks. Drinking too much, staying out late, and he dyed his hair black once during his goth phase, did he tell you? He looked like Dracula."

I looked at Max, trying to imagine him with jet-black locks. It was a struggle, his hair was so fine and fair.

Max buried his head in his hands and let out an embarrassed groan. "Don't mention that. And don't you dare get the photo album out."

"There are photos?" This was something I needed to see to believe.

"Somewhere." Andrea chuckled. "Next time I'm looking through the albums I'll put them to one side. Let's just say I'm glad that was a phase that passed quickly. It's a shame it coincided with a family wedding."

"You've got all this to look forward to," said Hector. "You'll see for yourself how much worry children cause when your daughter arrives."

"All worth it though?" I said, knowing the answer before Andrea gave it me.

"All worth it," she confirmed. "If I had my time again I wouldn't change a thing. Being a mum is the best thing I've ever done."

Her words were what I needed to hear, and what I already knew to be true. This baby was going to change everything, my life would never be the same again, but it was going to be the best thing I ever did.

As I leant my head against Max's shoulder I wondered what adventures our future held, what trials and tribulations life would throw at us. I couldn't wait to find out.

MARCH

Over the weeks I'd become a fully signed-up member of Iris's gang. No longer the tag-along, I actually felt like a part of their clique and looked forward to the times we got together to put the world to rights. I'd met their families, including their gorgeous tots who made me even more excited about the arrival of my own little bundle of joy, and although I still didn't have a clearly defined bump, my figure was changing. My hips were noticeably wider, my stomach more rotund, and I actually started to believe that I was pregnant. I'd known it from the moment I'd done the test, and my own eyes had seen the life growing inside me on the sonographers screen, but the physical changes in my body made everything seem that bit more real. That was why when Iris had suggested I visited Jessie's mum's baby boutique I jumped at the chance.

The shop itself was down a small alleyway, the window chockful of bold colours and patterns. I knew before walking through the door that it had the potential to be dangerous, and expensive. But, I reasoned with myself, I'd been so good at holding back on the baby purchases so far, the Babygro I'd bought with Eve and Tawna being the only item I'd bought new.

That's not to say I hadn't thought about buying things, there was so much temptation and when I went on the pregnancy forums online there were threads full of pictures of deluxe prams and debates about the benefits of Isofix car seats. I was well out of my depth, so going to see what was on offer with the help of my new friends was highly appealing. It might be a while before we were splashing out on the big stuff, but Max and I would have to start getting things together at some point and it paid to be informed.

"Excited?" Iris asked as she opened the door to the shop, bobbing so Jude bounced in the wrap of material that she was using as a baby sling.

I couldn't keep the smile from my face. I was stupidly excited to be looking at items that I'd possibly be using for my own baby. "I can't wait."

"Just a word of warning, my mum-in-law can be a bit opinionated," Iris said in a low voice. "She doesn't mean any harm, but sometimes she'll be very open about what she does and doesn't like."

"I'm sure I can handle her."

Iris's raised eyebrows acted as further warning, but I was too busy bubbling over with excitement to take heed. The teeny-tiny clothes hung on miniature white hangers were so adorably cute and the array of prams of all shapes and sizes, from simple buggies to space-age contraptions, were lined up in the window as though on parade. There were woollen blankets in rainbow colours, plain wooden toys and bright plastic teething rings; bibs and changing bags and something that looked like a potty that Iris swore was one of her best buys – a seat to help baby sit upright from when they could hold the weight of their own head. "We used ours all the time with Jude," she said wistfully. "Now he can walk it's redundant, until number two makes an appearance. But honestly, it was really useful."

I was admiring a soft giraffe print blanket (and planning ways to persuade Max that a jungle theme would work well in the box room-cum-nursery) when I could hear someone breathing over my shoulder. Scrap that, I could feel it, a warm wave of air against my neck.

I quickly turned, to find myself face to face with a formidable-looking woman with a dangerously eighties perm and a stern judgemental glare. It caused me to step back in shock, narrowly missing treading on a plastic bathtub much like the one I'd been given for free at the baby sale.

"Were you looking at the animal print?" the woman asked, her voice low.

It seemed a ridiculous question, it was quite obvious what I'd been looking at. I'd been stroking the fabric, checking the small white label to see what material it was made from (100% cotton). Something about her tone put me on edge.

"Erm… yes," I stumbled, this time with my words rather than my feet. "I like pattern and print and we already have a zebra print bouncer so…"

The disparaging look the woman gave me made me feel about an inch high. "There's no accounting for taste, I suppose." Her antipodean twang (and the cutting comment) made it obvious that this was Jessie's mum, owner of the shop and strong opinions.

I didn't quite know how to respond. There were two options – grit my teeth and be nice as pie, or turn into mouth almighty, which I had been known to be pretty good at on my day, and give her a piece of my mind. Given that I wanted to nurture my new-found friendships, I plumped for the former, although it was supremely tempting to reel off all the reasons why animal prints were the perfect design to have in a nursery, not just stylistically, but for nurturing baby's development. There's a whole market full of black and white toys and baby books out there for a reason.

"I'm an animal lover," I said, hoping that would be enough of an explanation. Never mind that it was a bit of a stretch – although I'd grown strangely fond of Scrat Cat, my neighbours' scruffy moggie who made a habit of climbing in through the window and pissing on my kitchen floor, I was no David Attenborough. I just liked the patterns of zebras and leopards and giraffes.

"There are some lovely blankets over here," she said, walking towards a wooden wall shelf stacked with neatly folded blankets in powder blue and ballet-slipper pink. She reached up and took one from the shelf, holding it out for me to touch. "And they're so soft. Merino wool, you see. Keeps baby warm in the winter and cool in the summer."

"It is very soft."

I rubbed the blanket between my thumb and forefinger. The motion was therapeutic.

That seemed to placate her and she visibly softened, deep-grooved wrinkles appearing around her eyes and at the pinched corners of her mouth.

"Do you know if you're having a boy or a girl?"

The question pleased me, because it suggested I must have actually been looking pregnant. Surely, even with her lack of tact, she wouldn't have asked such a question unless she was pretty sure I was a fully signed-up member of the club. She must have had plenty of people coming in to buy gifts for friends.

"A girl," I replied.

"Oh, I'm glad you're not one of those people who choose not to find out. It makes it so much easier for buying things if you know what you're having," the woman enthused, her doughy hand resting on my arm. "I know you youngsters all poo-poo the idea of pink and blue clothes, but it makes it so much easier for everyone to identify the sex. You don't want people asking if it's a boy or a girl, do you?"

She laughed, as though it was the most ridiculous thing in the world.

Iris sidled up to me, a rigid smile painted onto her face. "Don't pressure Sophie, Moira. She's a friend of mine."

A rush of happiness at being described as her friend ran through me.

"I wasn't pressurising anyone, Iris," Moira chided. "You know I'd never do anything of the sort."

I swallowed down a chuckle that was bubbling in my throat. From what Iris had told me about her mother-in-law it was exactly what Moira would do.

"We're only here to browse," Iris stated clearly, as Moira tickled Jude's cheek. The toddler giggled with glee. "Although if Sophie sees anything she likes then maybe she'll set up a gift list?"

She looked at me and I nodded. A gift list sounded like a good idea. Ever since we announced the pregnancy, people had been generously asking what we needed. We probably wouldn't need to buy much in the way of new stuff because with Nick and Chantel's hand-me-downs, mine and Mum's knitting skills and my charity shop habit, we'd most likely have everything we could need bar the dull stuff like breast pads. Still, it would be nice to have somewhere to send anyone who did want to splash out on a gift.

"Lovely," said Moira, reaching behind the counter for a clipboard and pencil and handing it my way. "Make a note of anything you like the look of and I can place it on the system. When you've finished browsing I'll take your details and give you a registry number." She shifted her focus to Iris. "Can I have a cuddle with my grandson now?"

Iris unwrapped the fabric, the swath of navy unfurling to the ground like a silks artist at the circus, and handed over her son. Moira was immediately coochy-coochy-cooing and bouncing the jolly baby on her hipbone, all attention on Jude.

"We'll just get on with looking around ourselves," said Iris, a tinge of annoyance in her voice, as we made our way towards the prams. Once we were out of earshot she added, "Sorry for Moira. She thinks she knows everything there is to know when it comes to motherhood."

"Must be annoying for you?" I said, sensing Iris needed a safe outlet.

"Just a bit," she answered with a grimace. "It's as though she can't give me and Jessie any space to get on with learning how to be mums ourselves because she's always got a pearl of wisdom or two for us no matter what the situation. I know I make mistakes, but I'm doing my best."

"Of course you are," I encouraged, trying to wash her insecurities away, "and you're a great mum."

"Thanks." Iris grinned. "Now, let's make a start on this wish list of yours."

I didn't need telling twice.

CHAPTER 14

"You've got a baby gift list?" Tawna frowned, as much as anyone who had frequent Botox sessions could frown.

"Is that a thing now?" Eve asked. "I know baby showers are really popular these days, but I've not heard of a baby gift list before."

Even though I knew she wasn't judging me, it felt as though she was. Eve wasn't the type to cast aspersions, but I still had a flash of panic that I'd done something wrong.

"It's just somewhere to send anyone who asks if there's anything we need for the baby," I said, shrugging off the uncomfortable tightening sensation in my chest. "We're not doing it expecting people to buy things, not at all, but if they want to then it means we'll get what we need rather than thirty newborn vests and a load of rattles that'll drive us nuts."

"Damn, and I'd got you a rattle as well," Eve deadpanned, which set Tawna off laughing.

"And I'd got you thirty vests," Tawna added with a wink, "with the baby sick, leaking nappies and endless drool I thought you'd need them."

"All right, all right." I rolled my eyes. "I know you think this is hilarious, but it's the done thing. It's no different to having a wedding list, when you think about it."

My friends must have been able to pick up on my frustration as they let it lie, but as they spent the whole mate date talking about home improvements and the new Michelle Williams film (which I'd not yet seen, being so wrapped up in baby-related excitement), I wondered if this was the start of our friendship falling apart for good. Over the years we'd weathered many storms – fights over silly things, like fancying the same boy and whether none of us should make a play for him or if it was a case of every girl for themselves. There had been times where we'd taken a step back from each other because of things going on in our respective lives. But we had always come back to each other, always, because we were tight. The three of us belonged together, like the musketeers, or the Chipmunks, or Busted. A duo just wouldn't be the same.

I worried this might drive a wedge between us though, because having a baby was such a huge, ginormous deal. Admittedly we'd cut back on the partying over the past eighteen months – Eve conscientiously saving for her flat and working towards the promotion she'd been dreaming of her whole life, Tawna spending more time at home doing whatever it was newlyweds did (I didn't like to think too hard on that) and me starting up my own sideline business selling my handicrafts online and at fetes and fayres, alongside falling in love and unexpectedly discovering I was "with child". It was a game changer beyond all game changers and from the look on Tawna's face every time I mentioned the baby (not to mention her constant need to remind me about the pain I'd be sure to endure during childbirth and how I'd be elbow-deep in dirty nappies for the next three years) I sensed her concerns about what we'd have in common by the time summer rolled around.

I'd been spending more and more time with my new mummy friends. It was easy to voice my pregnancy concerns around them, to garner their recommendations on the best baby groups in the city and the most popular schools (we'd have to move before baby started school, Max wasn't happy that our catchment school received an unsatisfactory OFSTED report). They understood what it was like to be overjoyed about pregnancy and simultaneously be scared half to death by the thought of having to give birth. They knew, they got it, in a way Eve and Tawna couldn't.

For the whole time we were together I was mentally switched off, instead thinking about later on when I was meeting Iris, Jessie, Rachel and Mia for tea.

♨

"So you met one of these women at a baby fayre?" Mum was snipping the stems of the bunch of flowers I'd bought her. With her birthday coming up I'd decided to treat her.

"Yeah. Iris, she's called. She's married to a woman called Jessie." I paused, wondering if Mum was going to make a comment about same-sex marriage. To her credit, she didn't. "They've got a little boy and their second baby's due next month. Then there's Mia and Rachel. Iris met them at antenatal classes."

"Good for you for meeting new people," Dad encouraged. "You'll be glad of your friends when the baby comes. It's a special time, but can be isolating. You found that when you had Sophie, didn't you, love?" he said, nodding in Mum's direction.

"What's that?" she said, shaken out of her stem-snipping-induced trance.

"I was just saying to Sophie that it's important to have friends around when you've got a new baby."

"It's the only time I've ever been grateful to have your auntie Trish round the corner," Mum said seriously. "I know she's a pain, but she used to bring me food to make sure I was eating properly, and told me everything I was missing out on. By the time I had Anna and Nick I knew what I was doing, but when it was just me and you I was petrified of leaving the house. The outside world seemed full of so many dangers that it seemed easier to stay home. The trouble was I put off even the simple stuff like going to the supermarket, and without realising it I cut myself off from everyone."

"I never knew any of this." I was surprised that my mum, who always seemed so together, could have had these worries. They sounded like a form of social anxiety.

"Why would you? It's not something I talk about," Mum said, filling a vase with tap water before pouring in plant food. "It was just a case of the baby blues."

She began arranging the stems of flowers, yellow and white chrysanthemums, and something in the way she avoided eye contact made me question why my mum living almost as a recluse after my arrival had never been mentioned before. Maybe that explained why our relationship had sometimes seemed strained. I'd heard of that before, where mothers and their babies hadn't been able to effectively bond in the early days and it impacted on their relationship.

"Anyway," Mum said finally, picking up the vase and placing it at the centre of the kitchen table, "tell me more about these new friends of yours. Did you say two of them are married to each other? How very modern."

The conversation about isolation was well and truly closed.

"I've never been so tired in all my life." Chantel knocked back her espresso as though it was a vodka shot. "The girls are driving me crazy with their tag-team sleeping, and although I love your brother he's useless when it comes to getting up in the night."

She rubbed at her eyes, the dull grey bags hanging beneath them indicative of her plight. Even her posture looked exhausted, as her shoulders flopped forward, her head bowed. It was as though her bones didn't have the strength to support her. It was enough to make me feel sorry for her even though her behaviour had been distant at best since me and Max had shared our news.

"Make him get up in the night," I said. "They're his children too. Just because he's going out to work doesn't mean he gets to wriggle out of the night wakings. Now you're bottle feeding he's got no excuses."

"That's easy for you to say, you're not at that stage yet." Chantel's tone, accompanied by an eye-roll, left me feeling small. "It's not even about the feeding or him getting up for work." Chantel sighed. "He doesn't hear them. Lord knows how, they sound like air raid sirens when they get going. My poor eardrums. I'm worried they might be permanently damaged."

"Surely he can hear them," I said doubtfully, knowing full well that my nieces' lungs were well-developed. They certainly knew how to scream. It's a good job they lived in a detached house or I'd pity the neighbours. I'd previously thought my nephew, Noah, was loud, but the girls beat him hands-down. "He's probably doing that thing where men pretend they're rubbish at something so women do everything. Max does that with the washing-up. He puts the plates on the drying rack when they're still crusty with food. It's gross, and I swear it's just so that I'll say 'don't worry about the washing-up, I'll do it'."

Chantel shakes her head. "With Nick it's not even that. He's really fast asleep. Even when I prod him he barely shifts an inch.

There's no way in the world he'd be able to get up and give them both their feeds."

"You need to put your foot down," I insisted, placing my hand on my stomach. "When this one arrives I'm going to make sure Max gets up in the night, I don't see why I should do it on my own."

Chantel gave me a wry, almost patronising, smile. "We'll see. It's different when they arrive."

She wasn't the first person to have told me that. I'd had words of wisdom from my mummy friends when I'd shared how I planned to raise my firstborn. They'd usually been accompanied by knowing glances and raised eyebrows, but I had a clear vision of how things were going to be.

"But you're so tired. You can't function on that little sleep."

"I'm certainly learning why sleep deprivation is used as a form of torture in some cultures," she said grimly. "All I can say is I'm glad we decided to send Noah to nursery three days a week, because if I had to look after him too it would be impossible. On the days he's at home he runs me ragged, because he wants me to kick a ball about with him or play a game. I'd love to be able to do it but I'm so bloody knackered that I can't. Never have twins, Sophie. It's exhausting."

"But they're beautiful." I looked across at my nieces. Imogen, who'd been the smaller twin at birth, was still a little dot of a thing, her woolly hat falling over her eyes whilst her sister Alicia's was a perfect fit. "When they're asleep like this it's hard to believe they're such awful sleepers at night."

"Everyone says that," Chantel said with a groan and a yawn. "They look like butter wouldn't melt when they're dreaming. It's in the middle of the night when they're screaming blue murder that they're testing."

"It won't last forever. They'll get into a routine and you'll forget you were ever surviving on three hours of broken sleep a night."

Chantel shook her head emphatically. "I'll never forget this. I love them both dearly and I wouldn't want to be without them, but I'm so drained. Half the time I don't know if I'm coming or going, I'm functioning on autopilot. I've got to drive because I can't get the bus with them in the double buggy and we're nowhere near the metro route, but I'm petrified of falling asleep at the wheel. I'm an accident waiting to happen. It's dangerous. And I'm sure I'm not the only parent who feels like this. How many people are there on the roads who can barely see straight because of lack of sleep?"

I smiled sympathetically, but did think Chantel couldn't be helping herself. I'd already started reading books on sleep training and planned to utilise the strategies suggested in them to ensure me, Max and the baby all got the much-needed sleep as soon as we possibly could. Maybe the lack of sleep was making her short-tempered and, well, short in general.

"You'll be fine," I said, reaching over and giving her arm a gentle rub. "Only eighteen years to go until they'll be off to university."

The words I'd hoped would make her laugh didn't have the desired effect. In fact, I'm sure tears of desperation welled up in my sister-in-law's eyes.

CHAPTER 15

Iris raised her eyebrows knowingly as I placed a pink and white spotted Babygro into my basket, the soft cotton fabric warm to my touch. It was the texture of the fabric which had drawn me to it.

"I thought you were against gendered clothing," she said.

"I'm not saying everything will be pink, but you have to admit there are some pretty things in here. And you know pink's always been my favourite colour."

We'd visited her mum-in-law's shop again to update my gift list. The tiny dresses called out to me from the hangers, looking impossibly small. They looked like they'd fit a mouse rather than a miniature human.

"They're lovely, but remember that babies grow quickly. What fits them one week is too small the next," she said, the voice of experience.

"I know. But look how cute they are!" I held up a floral print dress which was so adorable that I couldn't bear to put it back on the rack. "I'm not going to lose control, but I just want to buy a few really nice things. I'm excited."

"I know you are," she said softly. "And I know I told you

about this shop. But there are equally pretty dresses in the supermarket for a fraction of the price."

She cast a wary eye in the direction of her mother-in-law, fearful her words had been heard. Jessie's mother wasn't the kind of person you'd want to get on the wrong side of, and from my own previous experience I knew she could be overbearing.

"I'm just going to buy this one dress," I said, placing it against my bump as though trying it for size. The fabric easily covered the swell of my stomach, but I knew that by May it would be the perfect fit. I envisaged our daughter wearing it as Max pushed her around the park in a pram on a summer's day, where she'd attract an endless stream of compliments for her beauty from everyone who saw her. "It's too cute to leave. The other things I've seen can go on the gift list and I'll hope the grandparents are feeling generous," I said with a smirk, knowing my mum had already been unable to hold back from buying for her newest granddaughter.

Any fears I'd had about Alicia and Imogen diluting her excitement had been eradicated, if anything having two beautiful new babies in the family already was bolstering her excitement to uncontrollable levels.

Andrea was equally excited, asking us to share our thoughts on possible baby names, even though that was something we were keeping under our hat until birth day. We had a few shortlisted, but it would partly depend on what we felt suited the baby when we saw her. I'd always been a bit wary of those people who had a full name decided on before the birth, because what if the baby arrived and didn't look like a Holly or a Claudia or a Jemima? Would they be stuck with something that didn't suit them for the rest of their life? Or maybe we grow to fit the ones we are given, because Mum and Dad insisted that I was going to be a Sophie regardless, it was the only girl's name they could agree on. When Anna had arrived she'd been nameless for a fortnight as they struggled to find another girl's name they both liked enough.

After my excessive spending in the past I was cautious about staying in control and not allowing myself to go too wild, but this was my first child, and I wasn't going to feel guilty about buying something nice. So I took the dress to the till, gave my list of additional items to add to the gift list to Jessie's mum and wondered if I'd be able to hide the dress in the bottom of the wardrobe so Max wouldn't ask any questions. I didn't want to lie, but there was no harm in not telling the whole truth, was there? He'd been so proud of me for paying off my debts, through selling the designer clothes that had been part of my former life and the handcrafted items which were part of my current one. The Christmas stalls at fetes and fayres hadn't made me a millionaire, but had given me some business, and an article in the local press had helped too, directing traffic to my online store. It made me believe that I might not be stuck in an office forever.

As Jessie's mum handed me a brown paper bag containing the beautiful dress I couldn't contain my smile. It might be money I hadn't needed to spend, but I liked it a lot. Now I'd just have to find the perfect place to keep it safe, away from Max's gaze.

"So you've updated the gift list?" Eve was showing a real interest, her and Tawna having taken it upon themselves to host me a baby shower. Never mind that baby Oakley wasn't due to arrive yet, she had already fired off "save the date" texts to friends and family who'd attend the shower. "I'll need to let everyone know, in case they're planning on buying something from it for you."

"Don't you think you're jumping the gun?" Tawna said

warily. "It's still a long time to go until then, and Sophie might change what she wants for the baby in that time. You don't want people wasting their money."

I laughed at that comment, because wasting money was something Tawna Hamilton was an expert at. She loved nothing more than a day hitting the most-exclusive stores and spending money on her "personal upkeep" was a hobby. She'd try every lotion and potion, and although the perfume she always came back to was a popular brand, she made a point of layering it with the matching bath oils and body lotions so the scent lasted all day.

"We're not expecting anyone to buy gifts," I reminded her. "It's so we have somewhere to send them if people ask."

"Let her enjoy the moment, Tawna," Eve said disapprovingly. "There are so many lovely things in that shop I'm not surprised Sophie's added to her list. Even I was tempted to buy things and I'm not remotely broody."

"Just as well," Tawna muttered, and Eve pretended not to hear. She'd learned to turn a deaf ear to Tawna's not so subtle comments about her single status. "There's no sign of you settling down any time soon."

"Anyway," I said, drawing the word out in an attempt to change the subject, "fill me in on what's happening with you both. Eve, any progress with the house yet? And what's happening with the promotion?"

Eve's face visibly brightened. "The couple put in an offer and we've accepted, so it's a case of waiting now for all the surveys to go through." She placed her hands together as though in prayer. "I really hope we don't hit any stumbling blocks because I had an offer accepted on a flat the other day," she said, to oohs and ahhs from me and Tawna.

"I can't believe you didn't tell us," Tawna squealed. "What happened to the old Eve who blurted out gossip at the drop of a hat? I feel like I don't know what's going on in your life anymore."

"We're just busy," Eve shrugged, "and I knew I was seeing you today so I was saving it to tell you in person. And there's something else too..."

Tawna and I waited in anticipation.

"I got the promotion," she said, clapping her hands together excitably. "My dream job, leading the research team. I'll still be hands on, because you know I'd go mad if I was stuck staring at a computer screen all day, but it's more responsibility."

"That's amazing, Eve." I knew how much this meant to my friend, who'd worked so hard for this promotion. "You'll do a brilliant job, I know you will."

"Yeah, congratulations," Tawna said with a smile. "You must feel amazing."

"I do feel pretty amazing," Eve admitted in a hushed voice. She'd never been good at bigging herself up. "It's the role I dreamed of from the start, and I'll be the youngest person to ever manage a team there. All the other leads are men in their sixties," she said with a grimace. "However much we try and encourage women to work in STEM it seems the field is dominated by older men. Get your daughter into science, Soph," she teased. "Even it out."

"If she's got my genes then I doubt she's going to be Marie Curie," I said, naming the only female scientist I knew. "You know I was never any good at the academic stuff at school. I only passed Double Award Science because you helped me revise. You taught me everything I needed to know about photosynthesis."

"Which is nothing," Tawna said flatly. "When have you ever used that in real life? I wiped it all from memory the day I walked out of school for good."

"I use the basic principles of science every day," Eve replied drily, "so it's stood me in good stead."

"Well, yeah. I guess," Tawna said dismissively, although I knew deep down she was proud of our friend's achievements. "I suppose it has helped you."

"And we're really proud," I said, hoping Eve knew exactly how impressed we were. "Congratulations."

"I know it's not exciting to anyone else, but it's what I've been working towards ever since the day I started there. Before that really, from the minute I knew I wanted to work in science I was determined not to stay on the bottom tier."

"Exactly. That's worth celebrating," I said. "What are you doing on Friday night? Maybe we could all go out for drinks somewhere nice?"

I was thinking of the new cocktail bar that had opened near the river, and although I'd be firmly in the "mocktails only" camp, I was looking forward to a night together. Even though I'd been spending time with my new friends and loved having a group of women who knew exactly what I was going through, I didn't want to lose touch with Eve and Tawna. Our lives may have been going down different tracks but they were important to me.

"Sounds like a plan." Eve smiled. "I hear it's pricey but worth it."

Eve had been tightening her purse strings as she saved for her own flat, and it had coincided with my own life-changing saving mission.

"I'm not drinking at the moment," Tawna said, and both Eve and I gave her a sideways glance. Tawna was the biggest party animal out of the lot of us, so for her to make an announcement that she's tee-total, even in the short term, was a shock. "It doesn't mix with the medication I'm on," she explained.

"You never said you were ill," Eve chided. "What's up? Antibiotics?"

"It's the time of year for all types of nasty bugs," I said, crossing my arms in front of myself to ward off any germs. "Kath's been off work for a week with tonsillitis. She's on antibiotics too. If you're well enough to go out you can join me on the mocktails," I suggested.

"I'll manage it," Tawna replied bravely. "I'm fine, honestly."

"Good," I replied, looking at my watch and grabbing my bag when I realised my lunch hour was well and truly over. Marcie would be going nuts if I wasn't back at my desk soon, she was already in a flap about Kath being off. "I really need to dash though. Decide on a time and message me and I'll see you there."

I blew them a kiss as I hurried back to work, thinking how life was currently a crazy balance of the humdrum of work and the miracle of pregnancy. It was a very weird feeling.

CHAPTER 16

The mum group had convened at our house for an impromptu mid-week gathering to celebrate Rachel's birthday. "Not that being my age is anything to celebrate," she said. "I'm officially old now. Practically middle-aged."

"But you look ten years younger," I said, examining her blemish-free skin and gorgeous red hair. "No one needs to know how old you are unless you tell them."

"At the baby groups I'm the oldest mum by a mile," she said, her lips turning downwards. "Sometimes I wonder if it was selfish to have a child later in life. He'll probably be teased for having such a fossil for a mum."

"Don't be daft," Mia said. "You look amazing. And women have children at all ages, and the media make out they're wrong whatever age they are. Teenage mums are irresponsible and reckless, women in their forties are leaving it dangerously late, women in their twenties and thirties are causing chaos in the workplace because they want flexible working hours... I've come to realise there's no pleasing them. And heaven forbid a woman doesn't want children at all! They're made out to be freaks. Why can't there be less pressure all round and people just get on with living their lives?"

"Hear hear!" said Iris, raising her glass of non-alcoholic wine in a toast. "You're fabulous, Rach. We all are. To living our lives," she said chinking her glass against mine.

"To living our lives," we echoed.

"And balls to anyone who says we're doing it wrong!" Mia added empathically.

We'd just finished performing an out of key rendition of "Happy Birthday" when the doorbell unexpectedly rang. I hate it when people call unannounced, but there was no way I could avoid going to the door – the lights were on and it was obvious we were home. I winced with apology to my guests, stating if it was Jehovah's witnesses or cold-callers I'd send them packing as politely as I could.

I warily opened the door, fully prepared to launch into a spiel and get rid of whoever had the gall to interrupt our little party, but rather than anyone clutching leaflets or clipboards I was confronted by a delivery man dressed head to toe in a navy uniform carrying a large box.

"Hello," he said, his voice so cheery that I wondered if I was his last delivery of the day. "Package for Sophie?" he said, scrolling through the handheld device with a biro he was using as a makeshift stylus.

"That's me," I said, puzzled by what the box contained. I'd deliberately been cautious about buying things, knowing that once I was on maternity leave, money would be tight.

"You just need to sign here," he said, handing over the machine.

I scrawled my mark and he handed over the parcel, which was large but not heavy. Cumbersome.

"Thanks," I said, struggling to turn in the hallway with the box in my arms. I'd have to find somewhere to put it. If I left it in the hallway it would block the door, and Max would be back from the pub soon. He'd gone out with Iain, Oz and Archie when he'd found out the girls were coming over, and although I'd said he was welcome to stay I'd been quietly glad of a girlie night. Although he was understanding, I didn't want to talk about vaginal stretching or prolapses with him around, not if I wanted to have any kind of sex life after Baby arrived. Mia loved sharing the story of her birth, not leaving out any of the gory details. Max didn't need to hear that. He'd only worry.

After I closed the door on the delivery man I placed the box at the bottom of the stairs, peeling back the thick brown tape. Whatever the package held was hidden beneath hundreds of foam packing peanuts, screwed-up paper and half a roll of bubble wrap.

I could hear my friends in the room next door, giggling about something or other as I rummaged in the box, the soft foamy balls that were intended to protect whatever was inside lying out of the box and onto the carpet. Why did they make such a mess? I scooped them up and put them back in the box, even though I was desperate to see what the bubble-wrapped contents contained.

Picking at the Sellotape that had fastened the ends of plastic together, I tore it free, unravelling the protective packaging to find a layer of brown paper. Whoever had posted this was definitely not very environmentally friendly. The amount of excess packaging was insane.

Tearing at the paper, I saw a flash of material, a familiar giraffe print that I could recall what it felt like to touch just by looking at it.

My stomach flipped as the blanket from my gift list unfurled, and I checked the box for a delivery note.

But I already knew, could somehow sense, that there wasn't going to be one buried underneath the packaging, and my intuition was right. The laughter of my friends in the other room sounded louder, and in my heightened nervous state, made me feel ill at ease.

Whereas before I'd thought that whoever was sending me gifts may just have been forgetful, I was convinced they had their own agenda. There was only one reason anyone would send presents without saying who they were from, and that was because whoever was sending them didn't want me to know they were responsible. But who would do that? And why?

 could tell from the way he was looking at me that Max had doubts that I was free from culpability. Scepticism was etched on his face, and I almost wished I'd done what I had considered doing – disposing of the packaging in the bins without him knowing and giving the blanket to the charity shop. It would have been easier than trying to defend myself.

"It's fine to be excited," Max said, but there was a weary look on his face. "I expected you to buy things for the baby, and we can afford to get some nice bits as long as we don't go mad. I thought we could book the rest of the day off after you've been for the glucose test so we could choose things together. I'd like to be involved too."

"But it wasn't me that bought it!" My voice was screechy and wild, because it felt as though I could deny it a thousand times and Max still wouldn't accept that I had nothing to do with the unexpected deliveries. "Why won't you believe me?"

"It's a bit coincidental that this is the same blanket you've been talking about," he said, giving a look of disdain to it.

"How many times! The doorbell rang and there was a delivery guy waiting to hand it over. I knew nothing about it."

"Calm down," Max said, placing a hand on my shoulder as though to encourage me to sit. I shrugged him away, not wanting him to touch me when I was so angry with him. "It's not good for the baby for you to get worked up like this."

"You're the reason I'm getting worked up." My hands were curled into fists, my arms rigid with rage. "I've told you, I am as in the dark about this as you are. I don't know who's sending these things or why, but I don't like it. The first time I thought it could have been a mistake, but this time it's not."

Max's face softened. "I do believe you. I just think it's weird that we've had two parcels for the baby arrive unexpectedly and everyone we've asked about it has denied all knowledge."

"There is one person I've not asked that might do something like this," I said slowly. I'd been trying to squash down the possibility of Darius being involved, but this was exactly the sort of thing he would do, an overblown, misplaced and unwelcome gesture. My ex-boyfriend had never paid back the money he owed me from a trip when we were together, nor the money he'd wheedled out of me, pretending it was for his daughter. This was his style, all right. "Darius."

"No." Max shook his head. "He wouldn't do this... would he?"

"I don't know," I admitted. "He's a law unto himself."

"Does he know about the gift list?"

I shrugged again. "Maybe. Tawna and Johnny could have mentioned it. Or Nadia maybe."

This was the problem with the tangled lives we led, with how interwoven the fabrics of our being had become over the time our relationship had lasted. Darius and Johnny were best friends, which meant he'd be part of our lives as long as Tawna was a part of mine, and since I'd found out the truth about Darius's lies I'd become close to Summer's mum, Nadia, too. It was just a shame she lived in Liverpool, because she was exactly the kind of woman I needed in my life – sharp-witted and no-nonsense.

"It's a strange thing to do though, buy a present for your ex," Max said thoughtfully. "Unless he thinks by doing this he's paying back the money he used on the stag do."

"I could message and ask." I didn't really like that idea, because I tried to keep my distance from him whenever possible. It made for an easier life.

Max shook his head. "Let's just ignore it. I bet it's him and it wouldn't surprise me if he thought it was a way to get back in your good books."

That sounded a possibility. We'd had quite the falling out because I couldn't overlook how he'd lied about needing money to stay close to Summer when really he'd wanted it for himself.

"If that's what you want," I said, although the twisting in my stomach left me feeling uncomfortable. It wasn't that lovely warm sensation of our baby squirming happily inside me, instead it was the forceful knotting of angst and unease. Not knowing where the gifts were coming from gave me a sinister feeling of foreboding.

"I think it's for the best," Max said, placing his arm around my shoulder.

I exhaled slowly, allowing myself to melt into him. My shoulders loosened at his touch, and as I closed my eyes and concentrated on regulating my breathing, the aching in my neck ebbed away. If only my worries could dissolve as easily as the physical tension that had been building within me.

CHAPTER 18

"Don't you go lifting anything heavy." Eve shot a glare of warning in my direction. "In fact, why don't you just sit and watch? You can sort through some of the boxes. Unwrap the china for me?"

I'd helped her wrap it all up in newspaper, the crockery and tea sets that had lived in pride of place on Lucille McAndrew's kitchen dresser needed protection from the heavy-handed removal men taking Eve's possessions from the house she'd grown up in to her new home.

This was the first time I'd seen her one-bedroom flat, and it was all neutral-coloured walls and exposed lightbulbs, a stack of cardboard boxes piled in the corner of the open-plan living space.

"I want to be useful. I can do more than that."

"That would be useful," Eve said tenderly. "What I want more than anything is to make this place cosy. I know this is what I wanted – what I needed really, to be able to pay for Mum's care – but it's still alien to me. Having familiar objects around will help this place feel like somewhere I can call home."

I cast my gaze around the room. It was dull and grey, but the rainclouds which were clearly visible through the window weren't helping. On a sunny day it would be warm and bright, which would make it more welcoming. A work surface divided the kitchen area from the living space, where an alcove fitted out with shelving perfect for her science books, and paperwork, was tucked away in the far corner.

"I'm going to put fairy lights around there when I've got all my books organised," she said, as though reading my thoughts. "The books are one of the things I need to unpack first," she said, looking at the stack of boxes. I could see they were marked up in black felt-tipped pen, "KITCHEN" and "TOILETRIES" and "MUM'S JEWELLERY BOX". "These are the ones I need," she said, reorganising the boxes like Tetris blocks to find the ones labelled "BOOKS". She tried to lift one up, but it was obviously weighty, so instead Eve lowered to her knees and pushed it along to the alcove corner, guiding it around the settee. The action left tracks in the carpet where the pile had been pushed against the grain, the creamy colour looking darker where the box had travelled.

"Phew." As she wiped her brow she looked like she'd pushed the box much further than the fifteen feet from one corner of the room to the other. "One down, five more to go," she said, eyeing the other boxes.

"I could help."

"Don't you dare. I'll get you that box of china to unwrap and a bag for you to put the newspaper in so it can go out for recycling."

She used her fingernail to pick the tape from a box I could see marked "KITCHEN DRAWERS".

"I could have sworn I had black sacks in here somewhere," she muttered, as she rummaged through.

She pulled out a corkscrew, then a handful of flyers for local takeaways (I recognised a personal favourite pizza place's logo on one and instantly craved a large Meat Feast) before withdrawing a roll of bin liners.

"A-ha." She threw them to me and if it hadn't been for my quick reflexes they'd have hit me square on the head.

"Watch it," I said with a laugh, unravelling the roll and extricating one of the bags. "You nearly knocked me out there."

Eve carried a box across to me and placed it by my feet, stripping away the tape and revealing the contents – well-packaged plates surrounded by scrunched-up balls of newspaper to keep them safe. Seeing it reminded me of the parcel that had arrived a fortnight earlier, in a box similar to these. I'd half expected more items to arrive, but they hadn't, and although I'd questioned all the usual suspects again they'd all denied knowledge of the gifts. I'd even asked Iris, because although she was a new friend and I didn't think she'd splash out on such a lavish gift, she had been with me the day I'd first admired the blanket. She'd sworn blind she knew nothing about it though and I had no reason not to believe her.

"No lifting anything," Eve said firmly, as she squatted down again to push the second box of books towards the alcove. "Just carefully unwrap the plates and then stack them up."

"Yes, Mum," I teased, although it was nice to know she cared.

"You're the mum," she replied. "Or at least, the mum-to-be. That little girl is relying on you to look after yourself, and if her Auntie Eve can't help make sure she's in tip-top condition, then who can?"

"Message received, loud and clear," I said, raising my hand into a salute. "But I know she doesn't want her Auntie Eve to have a broken back either, so don't overdo it with those boxes, do you hear me?"

"I hear you." Eve pushed the box across the floor, the muscles in her arms flexing. "But I'll be happier when this lot's in order." She tapped the box fondly.

"You and your books." I shook my head but a smile played out on my lips. Eve had always treasured her beloved books, and this would definitely feel more like her own space when they were on the shelves. "Come on, let's get cracking."

I reached into the box and peeled back the layers of paper to reveal the dishes underneath. It was like an elaborate game of pass-the-parcel.

We busied ourselves in companionable silence, Eve occasionally humming to herself as she organised her books. By the time I'd unpackaged the plates and carried them (under Eve's watchful eye) to the kitchen area it was dark outside, and not only because of the gloomy north-east weather.

"Are you sure Tawna's coming?"

"She said she was." Eve shrugged, then checked her phone. "She's not messaged. Maybe when she said afternoon she meant evening."

"Maybe. When are we breaking to order takeaway?" I asked, suddenly ravenous. I hadn't eaten since breakfast.

"Another half an hour?"

I nodded. I could manage that. "And if Tawna's not here in fifteen minutes I'll ring to see if she's coming. Shall I wash these?" I asked, although I was already filling the sink with soapy water ready to soak the inky residue from the plates.

"Thanks, Soph." Eve smiled. "You're one in a million."

"Don't be ridiculous." I rolled up my sleeves. "All I've done is unpack a few boxes."

"You're helping me create a space where I'll want to spend my time," Eve said quietly, focusing on the books she was shelving, choosing some of her favourite titles to face cover-forwards like the books in the bookshop in town. I could hear her sniff, the first giveaway that she was upset.

"Hey, are you okay?" I threw the pair of rubbery yellow Marigolds onto the work surface and was at my friend's side in an instant. As I got closer I could see the tears in her large dark eyes, a sorrow hiding in them.

"Sometimes I get so lonely," she said, which only set her off crying even more. "I've been so busy for such a long time, first looking after Mum and then trying to get her place ready to sell, not to mention going for the promotion at work. It's like my brain's been churning all the time, mulling over everything, and now everything is as good as it can be and I still don't feel happy. Why don't I feel happy, Soph?"

"Because change is hard," I said kindly, draping an arm around her shoulder and tilting my head until my dull-blonde hair tangled with her black curls. "Anyone would be finding this tough. You'd lived in that house your whole life until yesterday, this is all new. It's a lot to take in."

"Everything about it is strange. What if I've done the wrong thing buying this place?" She moved her arm in a sweeping gesture. She sniffed once more. "It even smells weird."

"That's just because it doesn't smell like your air freshener or your perfume yet. It will, with time, and it'll feel more and more like home every day. You did the right thing," I said gently. "And it will get easier, I promise. Your mum's care can be paid for now and once you start gathering your own bits and pieces this will become a place you want to spend more time in."

"I feel so alone though," she said, dropping the book she'd been holding to the floor. "There's something so sad about a one-bedroom flat."

"Come on now, that's not true. You didn't think that when you first came to look at it, did you? You saw the potential and the freedom that having your own space would give you as a good thing. And it is a good thing, you're just having a bit of a wobble, that's all."

As Eve sank to the floor I sank down beside her, the two of us sat side by side, legs crossed, just as we had on Mrs

Mahoney's story time carpet in infant school, ready to listen to her reading chapters of the Famous Five books aloud each day.

"What are your dreams for this place?" I asked, trying to imagine what Eve would do once the last of the boxes had been emptied and flattened.

"I want to give the walls a lick of paint," she started slowly. "Something tasteful, maybe a pale grey with one dark feature wall."

"That's a good start. What else?"

"I'm going to hang the cross-stitch you gave me for my thirtieth on the wall in the hallway," she said, getting into her stride now, "and I want loads of plants. Spider plants, cacti, pots of herbs that I can use when I'm cooking..."

"Great ideas."

"I'm going to put up a curtain rail," she said, her voice laced with determination, "it'll make the room seem warmer if there are different textures. The blinds are okay, but it reminds me of the offices at work. Coming home to somewhere that reminds me of work isn't what I want."

"When you decide on a colour scheme I can run you up some curtains, if you like?" I offered, always glad of an excuse to get my sewing machine out and start making. "We could choose some fabrics and I could make cushion covers that complemented them?"

"And I want loads of throws," Eve said enthusiastically. "Then when I get in I can wrap myself up in a cocoon."

"That sounds heavenly."

"Thanks, Soph," she said, her voice cracking with emotion. "Not just for coming today, but for listening too. Everything seems less scary when I know I've got you supporting me."

A loud, unfamiliar, buzzing rang out all of a sudden, causing the pair of us to jump.

"That's the front door." Eve pulled herself onto her feet and pressed a button on the system on the wall. "Hello?"

"It's me," said a voice I immediately recognised as Tawna's. "Let me in. I called at the chip shop on the way over and they're going cold. It's bloody freezing out here."

"Come on up." Eve pressed the button to release the main door to the block so our friend could get in.

"Better get those plates washed," I said, pushing myself up in an ungainly manner. My bump might not be enormous, but my body didn't feel like my own any more, the weight distribution all wrong and leaving me unbalanced.

"Let's eat them the old-fashioned way," Eve said, standing in front of the gap that doubled as an entrance to the kitchen. "Chips taste better eaten straight out of the wrapping."

And that's how the plates were left to soak in the sink for far longer than planned, because when Tawna burst through the door larger than life, the vinegary scent filling the room, my mouth was watering so fiercely that I don't think I would have been able to dish the meal up without drowning in my own slobber. Anyway, I thought, as I licked the salt from my fingers, Eve was right. Chips did taste better straight from the wrapping.

CHAPTER 19

*A*s if helping Eve settle into her new place wasn't enough, Max kept dropping hints about finding a new home before the baby arrived. All his reasons for wanting to do this were right – my house was too small and not quite close enough to either his parents or my own for them to be immediately on hand. I also had the distinct sense he was keen for us to get away from the house I'd shared with my ex. Maybe it was jealousy rearing its ugly head, but Max insisted his reasons were purely practical.

"I've been online, just to see what's available," he said nonchalantly. "There's a place right near my mum and dad's that looks good, and it's got a huge garden."

"What do we need a huge garden for?" I laughed. "You've seen the sorry state of my plants. I'm hardly a landscaping expert."

"I was thinking of the future," he said, eyeing my bump. "Once she's on the move she'll need plenty of space to run about."

Part of me loved his enthusiasm, the other part wanted to

scream, "Give her a chance. She's not even born yet and you're trying to train her up to be a top athlete."

"Wanting to give our daughter the best possible start in life's not such a bad thing, is it?"

"I never said it was, but there's nothing wrong with the life we've got!" Sure, the eight hours a day I spent at the office weren't the most thrilling part of my day and although Max professed to love his job, I've no doubt he dreams of a more exciting life once in a while, especially now his closest friend's band is taking off. Max always said he had no interest in striving for a big-time career in music, but seeing the success they'd had – even being invited to play on one of the small stages at Glastonbury – must have given him a tinge of envy. They might not be headlining the Pyramid stage yet but still... Glasto was an achievement.

"Imagine what it'd be like to live somewhere like that though," he pressed. "Tree-lined streets, bigger houses, excellent schools..."

"We're a long way away from school applications."

It felt as though he was wishing our unborn child's life away already. Couldn't we get through the labour, the birth and the next four years first?

"I'm thinking ahead. We don't want our daughter to go to a failing school."

"My school didn't have a great reputation, but I turned out all right." I almost choked on the defensive words. "And Eve turned out amazing. She went to a run-of-the-mill comprehensive school too."

"You don't need to snap, I never said there was anything wrong with your education."

"You didn't need to. You implied it by saying we need to move closer to your parents and the la-di-da school you went to."

"It was hardly la-di-da." He laughed. "But the schools in that part of town are all in demand so they must be doing something right. I had a look at the OFSTED reports too and they're glowing. Besides you've got friends near there now. Rachel lives just down the road."

"We can't afford it anyway so I don't know why we're discussing it." I was keen to change the subject, aware of my blood pressure rising. It felt like my veins were being inflated with a bicycle pump.

"There's no harm in looking, I'm sure we could find a way. The house is already filling up with baby stuff and it's only going to get worse. You can barely get into the spare room as it is, let alone fit a cot in there. Think how nice it would be to have more space. If we got somewhere with three bedrooms, you could even have one for your crafts," he suggested, and I wavered at that. Having somewhere dedicated to creativity was appealing, and I'm sure Max knew that was the way to my heart. Since making the decision to take my craft more seriously and make it a small business, my stash of materials had multiplied. It didn't feel as frivolous spending money on wools and fabrics when I could write the expenditure in the little notebook I kept to record my incomings and outgoings ready for my tax return, but that did mean the plastic crates containing my stock and materials were taking over the place.

"How much is it per month?" I asked, softening to the idea.

What Max said next almost floored me. "It's not a rental, it's up for sale."

"Well, that puts an end to it. We can't afford to buy a place like that! Even if we could find a way to stretch to the monthly payments we wouldn't have enough for a deposit." I shook my head, wondering why Max thought it could even be a possibility.

"That's where you're wrong. Mum and Dad have offered to give us money for a deposit if we like it."

I didn't know how to respond. The words wouldn't come to mind let alone come out of my mouth. The revelation was so unexpected that I hadn't had chance to formulate an opinion, and although my head was thinking "that's incredibly generous" it felt as though people were trying to shoehorn me into a different life to the one I knew.

"Say something," Max encouraged, his eyes twinkling with excitement. His pupils looked enormous, the grey of his irises glistening like silver. "This is a great opportunity for us. No more playing at it, we would actually be living like adults. Let me show you the listing online." He pulled up an estate agent app on his phone and showed a picture of a large house. It wasn't as extravagant as the one Max's parents lived in, but the bay-windowed Victorian property looked far more grown up than our current Lego-brick new-build, even a step up from Mum and Dad's boxy sixties semi. My gut reaction was that I didn't deserve a home with such curb-appeal.

The thought that I was being pushed into this was still uncomfortable, my chest tightening as though a lead weight had been dropped on it. "I don't know. It looks really nice from the outside, but it might be a mess inside. The people who live there might be knee-deep in dirt."

"It's just as nice on the inside," Max assured. "There's a huge kitchen-diner that would be the hub of the home and a cosy living room with a wood-burning stove, plus a conservatory at the back. Three double bedrooms, one with an en suite. And a family bathroom, of course. You'd love it, Soph. It's even got one of those roll-top baths and a separate shower." The words tumbled from his mouth as though he couldn't keep them in. "And like I said, the garden's great. Flat, south-facing, big enough to add some decking even. I know you loved what Johnny and Tawna did to their garden last year. We could do something similar and still have plenty of grass for our daughter to play on.

And at the far end of the garden there's wild lavender so it smells amazing."

Something about the detail he was sharing niggled at me, it was too in depth, and he said it with a fervour that was hard to believe would be stoked purely by pictures alone.

"How do you know what the garden's like? There aren't any photos of it here."

"Ah." He gave me a sheepish smile. "I rang the agent to get more details. A house like that won't stay on the market for long. I thought that if I showed an interest and asked to be kept in the loop about any offers that went in we'd know if it was a possibility."

"You said the lavender smells amazing." The tightness in my chest was increasing, and I couldn't breathe properly. We'd had our fallings out in the time we'd been together and that had never bothered me – I was far more wary of the couples who insisted they never had a cross word to say to one another – but from the way he avoided my eyes I knew. He'd been to see this house without me. "How do you know that?"

"I had to go and look at the place. Yes, yes, I should have told you, but like I said it's not going to stay on the market for long and it was an itch I had to scratch. And I know it's a lot of money, but for that area it's a real snip. There's a communal green out the front, for crying out loud! The current owners are after a quick sale because they have sick relatives somewhere in Somerset and they need to move to look after them. Opportunities to buy a house like this don't come around often, not for people like us. That's why Mum and Dad said they'd give us the money."

"Please say you haven't put in an offer."

My heart was palpitating, I swear I had some kind of arrhythmic beat going on. What had happened to Max? The man I knew and loved was cautious and reliable, he wasn't the sort to make impetuous decisions. Although based on how he was behaving I was concerned that maybe I didn't know him as well as I thought I did.

"Not yet," Max said, and I breathed a sigh of relief. "But I've made an appointment for us to go and view it tonight."

I gave him what I hoped was a steely glare. How could he make such big decisions without so much as consulting me? I thought we were supposed to be in this together.

"Don't look at me like that, Soph. You're going to love this house, it's the perfect place to raise a family. I got carried away, I admit. But I'm doing it for us. For our daughter. There's nothing wrong with wanting to provide for you both, is there?"

"No, but we don't need to break our backs to get a big posh house. Haven't we got everything we need? We've got a roof over our heads, our families, each other, this little one's doing fine..." I stopped to rub my stomach. Baby kicked in response. It made me feel as though she was on my side.

"I don't see the problem in having aspirations for more. We're lucky, but our child deserves the best."

"Which doesn't mean we need to overstretch ourselves," I snapped. "Both of us have overspent in the past and we're only just getting back on our feet. I'm going to be off work for at least six months and we'll be reliant on your wage because maternity pay isn't going to go far. The timing of this is terrible."

"Hold off judgement until you've been to see it. I promise you'll be blown away. There's nothing that needs to be done, it's immaculately decorated, but there's potential to extend upwards into the loft in the future. Please don't be mad at me for being excited. When you come out of there tonight I guarantee you'll be as in love with it as I am."

The light in his eyes as he spoke about the house scared me. Could this house drive a wedge between us? The way he batted away my financial concerns and couldn't see why I was upset that he'd been to see the house – and presumably spoken to his parents about it, asking for a loan – made it seem like a done deal. His enthusiasm suggested that in his head he'd already moved in, but I couldn't rid myself of the discomfort. It didn't sit well. It didn't sit well with me at all.

CHAPTER 20

The minute I saw the house, I knew. The way the March sun reflected from the panes of glass in the pale green front door it was as though it was beckoning us in. My body seized up with the realisation my resolve was floundering.

"You can see why I fell in love with it, can't you?" Max whispered as we were ushered into the house by the estate agent. Sweeping high ceilings greeted us in the hallway along with the varnished parquet floor I'd always secretly dreamed of.

"It's lovely," I admitted, poking my head around the door of the living room, which revelled in a glut of original features. The wood-burning stove was the focal point of the room, but looking up I was entranced by the cornicing and an exquisite ornate ceiling rose.

Each room was better than the next, the enormous kitchen-diner a room I could imagine nursing the baby in as Max put his own twist on recipes he'd downloaded from the BBC Food website. The south-facing conservatory was light and bright and would make a perfect playroom, leading straight out onto the long garden which seemed to go on forever, only broken by an apple tree with an old-fashioned string-and-plank swing. In the distance the faded purple sprigs of lavender Max had mentioned caught my attention.

Even the smallest bedroom was a decent size and would make the perfect craft room, especially as it boasted a ready-made storage solution – a walk-in cupboard with built-in shelving.

And the master bedroom was a delight, with a wrought-iron fireplace and a sparkling-new en suite. "They only put it in last summer," the agent said. He must have picked up on my keenness. "Tasteful, isn't it? And good to have an alternative to the main bathroom."

And oh, the bathroom! It looked like it belonged in a spa hotel rather than a family home. It even had that smell, the fresh, faintly salty smell, that you found in a spa.

"You'd be able to come home and have a well-deserved soak at the end of the day," Max said with a smile as I looked longingly at the roll-top bath. "Lots of bubbles, a few candles, a glass of wine..." His voice trailed off and I knew he'd won me around. This house would be ideal for us. It was everything that I'd ever hoped for, the wildest dream in a house-shaped package.

"Think how much it's going to cost though," I said, trying to keep a hold on my emotions. In the past my heart had ruled my head and it had ended up with me running up a five-figure credit card bill. "We've got to be sensible. The mortgage on this place must be twice what we pay in rent."

"We could manage, Soph. I know we could. And if we don't take a chance now, we're going to miss out. Houses like this don't come around very often, and definitely not at this price."

"I know, I know. And I don't want to be miserable about it, but I'm trying to be the voice of reason. What if interest rates go up? No one knows what's going on with the economy since

Brexit." My knowledge of the economy was patchy at best, I was just regurgitating what I'd heard on the TV. "And babies are expensive. When I go back to work nearly all my wage will go on childcare. I've heard Mia and Rachel talking about how much they're paying, and it's daylight robbery."

"If you go back to work," Max said, and I looked at him in puzzlement. "You're always complaining about it, and if it's not bringing in any money, then what's the point? You could be a stay-at-home mum."

He was right. There were many times I'd complained about the monotony of my day job and how thankless it was, especially when I had a grumpy lawyer telling me the notes I was typing up should have been done the day before and the client I was chasing up payment from kept making excuses. I'd often remarked how I'd love to jack it all in, but now Max was suggesting it I wasn't sure anymore. My job might not be much, but it was a part of my identity, and the close bond I shared with my workmates had got me through many a tough time.

"I could speak to my boss about opportunities for promotion," he continued, oblivious to my concerns. "The area manager we've got at the moment is mediocre at best. I could do as good a job, if not better. Maybe they'd consider me if they're looking for a replacement."

"We can't buy a house on a maybe."

"When we get home let's do the maths. I know we can find a way to make it work. My savings are there to dip into with good reason and this is as good a reason as any."

The estate agent joined us. "Have you seen enough or do you need a bit longer?"

"I think we've already decided we love it," Max said. "We'll be in touch in the next day or two."

"Excellent. We've another two viewings booked in tomorrow

morning and it's priced to sell, so if you decide to make an offer I'd do it soon."

"Oh, we will." Max held out his hand.

The estate agent reached out and shook it. "I'll look forward to hearing from you."

The salesman walked one way and we walked the other, heading towards Max's Mini.

"Let's go and crunch the numbers," Max said, reaching out and squeezing my hand. "This house is meant to be ours, I can feel it."

Although the house was perfect, almost too perfect if I was being honest, I couldn't stop worrying about making a commitment that might be stretching our finances too far. Life was already about to change monumentally. Was I ready to be a homeowner too?

"I know that road!" Iris exclaimed, bouncing Jude on her hip. "It's gorgeous."

"I know." There was a hint of smugness in my voice that I didn't even try to hide. "And it's not far from some lovely independent shops and cafés." I'd allowed myself to daydream about pushing the pram along the streets, saying hello to all the neighbours who would no doubt become great friends, and enjoying a latte and slice of cake in one of the independent eateries.

"What a lovely area to live in," Iris said. "I dream of a place like that. I've been in Rachel's house and it's stunning, but the area is the real selling point."

The location had won me over in the end. As beautiful as the house was and as much as I could envisage us making it our family's nest, it had been the good schools that convinced me, that and how it had an active neighbourhood watch group. Since finding out I was pregnant, safety had become a top priority.

"I'm on tenterhooks waiting to hear from Max," I admitted.

He'd phoned first thing to put in an offer. Not quite the full asking price, but we hoped that wouldn't count against us. We weren't trying to be cheeky, but after poring over our incomings and outgoings we'd come to an agreement about the bid we could realistically put forward.

"I'll bet. It's a big deal. This could be your family home."

"Do you think we're crazy? If they accept the offer it'll be getting close to my due date before we'd complete."

"Sometimes a little crazy is a good thing."

I gave her a look.

"No, really. Life is full of moments where we have to decide whether to take the sensible path or take a risk. The risky path isn't always as big a deal when you look at it with hindsight."

"If only I could time travel forward five years to see if we're making the right decision," I said with a thoughtful smile. "I don't want this to be a massive mistake."

"What's the worst that could happen?" Iris cupped a mug of herbal tea. "If you decide you hate the house, you move. If the mortgage repayments are too expensive, you move. You've said yourself that this house is a bargain, so I bet you'd make a profit on it."

"You make it sound so easy."

"It is easy." She took a sip from her mug before resting the half-empty cup on the table. "Most choices in life are reversible. Think of your life a few years back, and I'll bet you anything it's changed since then."

She didn't know about the overspending in my past, but Iris had struck a chord. My life had changed beyond all recognition. Life with Max was almost the polar opposite of how it had been with Darius. Everything that had been the "normal" in my twenties, such as nights out on the lash and spending extravagantly on beauty treatments and make-up that promised to change my life had been shelved. After the initial super-strict period at the start of my saving I had allowed myself monthly eyebrow and bikini-line waxing, because they were things I really missed, and I did pay out to get my hair cut once every three months, but I'd stopped the ridiculous highlights and changed from a top-priced salon to the hairdresser my mum used. It wasn't as smart, but at a third of the price it was a saving well worth making. So much had changed, and even the things that had seemed so awful at the time were nowhere near as bad in retrospect.

"More than you could know," I said, as my phone rang. The ringtone caused me to jump, it seemed unnaturally loud. "Do you mind?"

Iris shook her head.

"Hello," I said, my voice tentative when I saw it was Max who was calling. "Any news?"

"It's ours, Sophie! It's ours!"

"No way! They accepted the offer?" It had seemed such a long shot that I'd been mentally preparing for the rejection. I looked over at Iris who smiled, clearly having got the gist of the conversation.

"They turned down the first offer but said if we could go up by five thousand and push to complete within six weeks they'd accept it. It's coming off the market right now and no one else will view it. They really were just after a quick sale."

His words rang in my ears. "You offered an extra five thousand? Without even asking me?" My voice wavered. Yet again Max was surprising me with his actions, and not in a good way. Making such enormous decisions without consulting me made me feel like a fifties housewife, a kept woman. First he was talking about me giving up my job, and now this.

He must have picked up on my discontent, because he sounded mildly snippy as he replied, "That's what had to be done to make sure it was ours, Soph. There wasn't time to call you, I had to make a decision on the spot. And it's what we both want, what we need to do to give our child the best start."

I thought of Iris and Jessie, living in a council house in one of the dodgier parts of Newcastle. Was I being ungrateful? Even though I was put out by his behaviour, Max was doing this with the best of intentions. It was because he loved us, me and the baby. A primal caveman instinct had kicked in and he'd taken on the role of protector and provider.

I couldn't cause a scene, not here in this civilised little café with frilly lace curtains and white-haired women putting the world to rights over a shared pot of tea, and not in front of Iris who was gazing at me with expectant eyes. I mouthed a "sorry" but she shook her head.

"Our house," I muttered quietly into my phone, trying to absorb it. It was one thing looking around it and daydreaming, it was going to be something else entirely heading back there after a day at work and knowing it was ours. "Our home."

"I know you're worried about the financial side of it but I promise you we can manage. And we won't have to spend on decorating. We can move straight in when it all goes through. It should be quick, which works out well for us."

I did a bit of mental arithmetic. Six weeks would take me to thirty-five weeks pregnant. That would give us a month to make it our own, ready for when we brought Baby back from hospital.

"I hope they're right. I don't want to be the size of a whale when we're moving and my bump's getting bigger every day."

"You won't have to lift a finger," Max promised.

I didn't have the heart to say that wasn't what I wanted. This was a huge deal, a major life event. I wanted to take an active part in it, for it to be something I made happen rather than something that happened to me.

"We'll talk later," I said, vowing to find a way to voice my concerns about Max going into autopilot.

"We've got so much to plan. This is the start of something brilliant for us. We've just bought a house, Soph! Our forever home!"

And although his words set off a fizz of excitement within me, there was a pang of sadness too. It didn't feel as though we'd just bought a house. It felt as though Max had.

CHAPTER 21

I was dreading the conversation but knew I had to be brave. What should have been a happy time was overridden by the sense of being a bystander in my own life.

My mouth was so dry and my constant lip-licking was making my already-chapped lips sorer still, but I couldn't help myself. It was the only thing that calmed me down enough to believe I'd be able to tell Max exactly how I felt.

"Come on, Sophie," I said to myself, jiggling my shoulders, hoping getting blood moving around my body would enable me to face up to the difficult situation. "You've got this."

Max's key rattled in the lock, the sound of metal on metal setting me on edge in the same way fingers down a blackboard would.

I clasped my hands tightly together.

"Hiya," he called. "I'm home."

"Hi," I replied tersely, wriggling myself off the sofa in the ungainly way that had become my new normal. There was no point trying to delay this conversation.

He was unwinding his striped scarf from around his neck as

I caught sight of him, his cheeks red from where the wind had slapped against his skin.

"We need to talk about the house," I said.

"I know!" A gigantic grin spread across his face. "We're going to be busy over the next couple of months. I've already contacted a mortgage advisor – it's someone my dad knows and will make sure we don't get ripped off – and I thought you could speak to someone at work about the surveys and stuff."

He looked at me hopefully.

"We specialise in family law not conveyancing," I reminded him. It irritated me that he had to be reminded.

"They can recommend a firm who'll do a thorough job though, can't they?" He shrugged out of his coat and draped it over the back of one of the dining chairs. That annoyed me too, there were coat hooks in the hallway and even one of those metal hangers that hooked over the door so they weren't piled on top of each other. That he couldn't be bothered to use them made me cross.

"I know who does a good job," I hissed, inwardly seething. "We get tons of calls from people who don't know what we do and I direct them all to Morgan, Morgan and White. Morgan Senior studied with Vernon," I said, naming the eldest partner at the law firm where I'd worked longer than I had at any other job.

"We'll call them, then, make sure they can get the ball rolling. If we want this to happen quickly there's no time to be messing about."

When I didn't respond, Max caught my gaze. My irritation must have been apparent in the hard line of my lips, because he said, "What's up, Soph? You're not getting cold feet, are you?"

He reached out to put a hand on my shoulder, a hand I knew was meant to offer comfort and make me feel better, but only made me tense further. I didn't want to be touched, I wanted him to realise that the way he'd railroaded me over the past twenty-four hours was out of order.

"I'm not getting 'cold feet' as you so quaintly put it," I snapped, adding angry air quotes to convey my pissed-offness. "I haven't had a chance to get cold feet, you've been so busy pushing me into this. This time yesterday you were suggesting going for a viewing and now we're halfway towards owning a house in one of the most desirable postcodes on Tyneside. And don't even get me started on you offering more than we'd agreed on without so much as calling me. That speaks volumes about how much my input into this relationship counts."

Max's mouth was slack, his knitted eyebrows looked as though they were balancing on the upper rim of his glasses.

"I thought it was what you wanted." His voice was low and calm. "I wasn't doing it to be controlling, I was doing it for you."

I wished he'd rant and rave like I had, but Max wasn't that kind of person. The few times we'd argued it had always been the same – he built a protective wall around himself. He'd told me it was a result of being previously hurt.

"But I never asked you to do it."

"I saw how much you loved that house. I know you were imagining everything we'd do with it if it was ours." Genuine confusion was etched on his face as he added, "You were talking about making apple crumbles in the autumn with fruit from our own tree."

"Getting carried away with a fantasy doesn't mean it's what I want!" The frustration manifested as a high-pitched squawk. "What I want is a partner who'll talk to me before making life-changing decisions!"

I was nigh on hysterical, the tension in my face making me dizzy. Clenched teeth. A pulsating in my temples. All the signs of a migraine brewing inside my skull.

Although I was raging I had enough sense to pull out a chair, the same one Max had sloppily put his coat on, dragging the wooden legs along the lino and not caring that it would probably leave a mark. The coat fell to the floor, landing in a crumpled heap. I didn't care about that either.

Stars flashed before my eyes, like chips of diamond reflecting the bright spotlights embedded into the ceiling. I instinctively grasped the side of the seat, my hands turning into vice-like claws gripping onto the wood.

"Take a breath." Max's voice was muffled, and I could see him, fuzzy around the edges as though in soft-focus. "Breathe in, breathe out. In, out."

I wanted to stay mad, but my head felt as though it was going to burst with the pressure building inside it. This couldn't be good for the baby. I forced myself to inhale through my nose until the air was in my mouth, in my brain cells.

"That's better," he said soothingly, as I loosened my grip on the chair. "Stay calm."

"This isn't a get out for you, Max. I'm still angry. We're meant to be a partnership, equals. That means trusting each other, being honest. No more secrets, right?"

Max nodded. "I promise, no more secrets."

APRIL

My irritation decreased as excitement took over; each step of the process taking us closer to being the proud owners of the house on Anderson Green. The vendors were as keen to move as they'd said they were, pushing for the surveys to be completed as quickly as possible and giving fast responses to any queries. I'd informed the letting agents we'd be leaving and had started packing. Even though I'd sold my surplus belongings, I still owned a lot of stuff. That said, me and Max would be rattling around once we got to the big house, because we wouldn't have enough to fill it.

"I've never seen so many boxes as I have in the last month," Tawna exclaimed. "Everyone's moving at the moment. I know they say spring is when everyone's meant to put their houses on the market, but it feels like we're still in the depths of winter." She peered out of the window, which would have benefitted from a good wash, truth be told, watching the clumpy flakes of April snow swirl on the wind. Since she'd arrived the snowfall had gone from a delicate dusting to a full-on blizzard. "It's almost enough to get me thinking about putting the house on the market."

I gave Tawna a look. "Don't be daft. Why would you want to move? Your house is amazing."

"Don't get me wrong, I still like it and Johnny wouldn't want to move, not now we've got it how we want it." They'd extended up into the loft, creating a beautiful bedroom which reminded me of upmarket hotels – the white walled space filled by a king-sized bed, a small table with a vase of fresh, fragrant flowers and a loveseat – and a spacious office to replace the small downstairs one Johnny had previously worked from. Although he was usually based in the city centre and the company offices, I knew my friend's husband often came home with business he "had to wrap up". That's the thing about Johnny, he played hard but worked hard too. "Anyway," she continued, "I'm looking forward to the summer. I love being able to have our tea out on the decking with nothing but the sounds of the breeze in the trees and the baby birds cheeping."

She looked out at the snow once more and I wondered if she was suffering with SAD. People found the long, dark winters difficult to deal with, I knew that, and Tawna was the kind of person who embodied everything that was summer. She liked pretty sandals and dresses with spaghetti straps, not woolly knitwear and winter boots. Perhaps that was why she'd seemed so distant lately, the winter had dragged.

"I can't get my head around the fact we're actually moving. Everything's changing so fast I feel almost as though I need to take stock. Antenatal classes start tonight."

"Whereas my life is dull and predictable," Tawna said with a dramatic sigh.

I had to stifle a laugh, because there was nothing about Tawna's life that was dull. She'd been out again at a business award's do at the Vermont just the night before. I'd seen the photos on Facebook, my friend looking stunning in a floor-skimming silver gown with a steel-grey fake fur stole, a suited and booted Johnny by her side. I'd say the pair of them scrubbed up well, but that did them a disservice. They didn't need to make an effort, the winning combination of good genes, dazzling smiles and well-cut clothes enough to make them appear film-star glamorous. The hint of a snicker that escaped must have alerted Tawna to my amusement at her comment.

"What?" There was a prickliness to her tone. "It is. Every week is the same and I'm sick of it. You might look in from the outside and see a young married couple with everything going for them, but there's no excitement in my life anymore." She sighed. "Monday I go to the nail bar. Tuesday I visit my mum. Wednesday is spray tanning. Blow-dry on Thursday. We go out on a Friday and Saturday, for a meal one night and something business related on the other. Can you blame me for being bored out of my mind?"

"You could get a part-time job?" I said tentatively. "It'd give you something else to focus on."

She shook her head. "Not an option." There was a dangerous look in her eyes that stopped me from challenging her.

"Or a dog? Anna and Jakob dote on theirs," I said, thinking of the cheeky-faced French bull terrier puppy my sister and her husband had recently bought. They treated him like a baby, even including him (dressed in a miniature Santa suit, obviously) on the photograph they sent out with their Christmas cards.

"Too much of a tie," she said, picking at the skin around her nails. Good job it was a Sunday and she'd be making her weekly trip to the nail bar tomorrow. "And all that walking. Next door are always wrestling theirs into the Range Rover to take it down to the lake. They're out for hours at a time, every day."

"They do have a St Bernard," I pointed out. "You could get

something small that wouldn't need much exercise. A Chihuahua maybe? I could see you with one of those. You'd be like Reese Witherspoon in *Legally Blonde*."

She screwed up her nose judgementally. "They look like rats."

"Okay, a sausage dog then. They're cute."

"They are," she conceded, "but I don't think me and Johnny are ready for that right now. Things are busy."

I looked at her quizzically. She'd only just been bemoaning the lack of excitement in her life and now she was complaining she was too busy.

"Johnny's got a lot on at work," she explained. "They've just taken on a contract to build a new estate on the outskirts of town." She carried on talking, sharing the location and how much pressure Johnny felt after snatching the contract from the jaws of the national companies who specialised in new builds. Until now Johnny's success was very much regionalised, but from what Tawna said, his ambitions were to expand.

"That sounds exciting to me. He's going great guns."

"You know what Johnny's like, he's all work, work, work and he's not the sort of man who'd give up. Once he sets his mind on something he gives it his all and that's what's happened with this project. I'm just glad it's paid off for him." Her words were proud but there was still a sadness in her eyes.

"Me too," I said with a smile. "If anyone deserves success it's Johnny."

"He puts in the hours, but it does mean I'm spending a lot of time waiting for him to get home."

"What you need is a hobby," I said, a flash of inspiration taking over me. "I know you and Eve thought it weird that I spent so much time crafting when me and Darius split up, but it was the only thing that kept me sane. Knowing I had something to occupy me when I went home to an empty flat was a relief. And I didn't realise it at the time but that was the start of my business. It was a blessing in disguise."

"How's it going?"

"Things have slowed down since the Christmas fayres, but online sales are steady. It was definitely worth handing out business cards. Some people think they're old-fashioned, but customers pick them up and take them away and hopefully they'll remember me in the future. I had a couple of emails asking for custom orders too." I'd knitted a matinee jacket in a bright red wool for a lady whose husband was a big Manchester United supporter (I wish she hadn't revealed that – I've never been a fan and have clear memories of them thumping Newcastle in one of the first matches I ever went to).

There had been another commission too, to make a memorial necklace for a woman whose mum had passed away. That had been an honour and I'd threaded each rainbow-coloured bead with all the love in my heart. My relationship with my own mum may have been fractious at times, especially when I'd convinced myself she was comparing me to my over-achieving siblings, but the truth of the matter was I couldn't imagine life without her, especially now I was about to become a mother myself. She'd been a great supporter of my business too, taking my home-made Christmas cards door-to-door when she did her Avon round. She was quite the persuasive saleswoman, selling more cards than I could have dreamed.

"I could teach you how to knit, but I'm not sure that's something you'd be bothered about learning."

Tawna's mouth fell open. "Knitting? Me?"

"Sure, why not?"

"I can't even sew a button on when it falls off so what chance have I got of making anything worth having?"

"It's not all about how it looks in the end. The process is really therapeutic, it helps with stress."

"It's easy for you to say, you know how to do it. Something like that would only get me all worked up. You know I hate it when I feel I can't do something."

"It doesn't have to be knitting, that was just a suggestion. You could do anything! Cupcake decorating, mountain biking, trainspotting..." I had a chuckle to myself at the thought of Tawna standing on a platform at the station wearing a waterproof rain mac as she scribbled down train numbers. "Maybe not trainspotting. But you've got options. What would you do if you could do anything?"

"I'd like to learn floristry," she said slowly. "When I was organising the wedding I loved looking at the spreads of bouquets in the wedding magazines and visiting the florist to share my ideas. The lady there was really helpful, telling me what was in season and which flowers were most likely to date in the photos."

It was the most animated I'd seen her in a long time, so I was keen to encourage her. "You could do that, I bet the college runs beginner's courses."

I pulled out my phone and typed "Newcastle college floristry course" into the search box. A list of options popped up and I clicked on the top link before handing my phone to my friend.

Tawna scrolled in silence, although her lips moved as she read. It was an endearing habit she had.

"So?" I asked eagerly. "What does it say?"

"There's a course starting in six weeks' time," Tawna replied, a sense of excitement in her voice. "It runs every Monday for twelve weeks. Enrolment's open now."

"You should go for it." Maybe this would reignite my friend's spark. "This might be the excitement you've been looking for."

I thought a glimmer of darkness passed over her face, but then she smiled at me. "Maybe. It'd keep my mind busy."

"So you'll register?"

"I'll think about it. Thanks, Soph. Thanks for caring."

I reached out and placed my hand on hers. "I'll always care about the happiness of my friends."

CHAPTER 23

*H*aving decided against NCT classes in the end (because as I already had a group of mummy friends to offer advice it didn't seem worth forcing friendships) Max and I were attending the NHS antenatal classes at the local clinic, a building with pockmarked vinyl flooring, cheap plastic blinds and a strip light with an annoying tendency to flicker.

Eight other couples were sat on the same plastic chairs, everyone shifting uncomfortably – the pregnant ladies because the seats were hard and not particularly wide, the partners because they weren't sure what to expect.

The midwife at the front of the room had been setting up her resources as we arrived, everything from baby bottles to knitted breasts and, somewhat scarily, a life-sized model of a uterus with a baby that looked far too large for the space it was confined in.

After the usual welcomes and cringe worthy ice-breaker exercise (I don't think I needed to know that Jill's unusual craving of munching on lumps of coal is actually a common one and that some people think it indicates an iron deficiency) the business begins.

"Let's start by talking about labour because that's when your journey into parenthood really gets going. The next session will be a tour of the hospital including showing you our labour suites and the birthing pool. Today we're going to cover pain relief options and I know from the forms you returned to book onto the course that some of you are interested in alternative therapies to use alongside or instead of medical options."

She carried on talking, producing all kinds of props to aid her presentation – the scary model, a pair of forceps (which looked like supersized serving spoons), a canister of gas and air with a mouthpiece which the midwife mimicked taking deep breaths through. There were essential oils, homeopathic remedies, an in-depth explanation of what happens during the administration of an epidural. She spoke of home births, water births, active births and hypnobirthing. There was so much to take in and what with the information overload and the flickering light I was worried I might have a migraine.

Thankfully the next activity was far more relaxing.

"Some women respond to massage during labour," the midwife explained, "which is why we always teach birthing partners a few basics."

The five minutes that followed involved a simple shoulder and back massage, and the circular actions of Max's thumbs against the base of my neck certainly aided my relaxation, even if the lady next to me was squealing with giggles every time her partner touched her.

"Sorry," she said, cheeks red with shame. "I'm ticklish."

After the touchy-feely session we moved on to baby care, starting with how to change a nappy followed by the midwife using a doll and the knitted boob (which was way smaller than my current weighty boulders) to demonstrate the best positions for breastfeeding.

Although the midwife had been positive and full of

motivational speeches, there was still a flutter of nerves in my stomach as we left the clinic. There was so much to remember, and this was only session one. Besides the follow-up including the hospital tour there was also a baby first-aid course that I'd insisted me and Max enrol on. As if we weren't busy enough!

"Come on. I'm taking you out for tea. The last thing we need is to be cooking after that. Let's go to that pub on the roundabout that does those pies you like."

I could have kissed him, and would have, except I'd already inelegantly clambered into the back of the car so I could stretch my legs across the whole width of the car by sitting diagonally. Never mind Jill and her weird coal craving, I was lusting after a steak and kidney pie with chunky chips and mushy peas.

"You must have read my mind. And pudding. We've got to have pudding."

"Chocolate brownie and ice cream?"

"How did you guess?"

Max chuckled affectionately. "You always have the same thing."

"Because I know it's good. If I had something else it might not be as nice and I'd be regretting not having the brownie."

"Which is why," he said, "you shall indeed have pie, chips and peas followed by brownie and ice cream."

"I feel like I need a glass of wine as well after that. These classes are supposed to be helpful, so why am I more confused about what I want than before? I hadn't even thought of half of that stuff. How do I know if I'll want to be sniffing on a cotton wool ball soaked in essential oils? I've never done this before."

My voice quivered and a concerned Max peered over his shoulder at me as we waited at a junction.

"You don't need to worry. I know it's easy for me to say because I'm not the one who'll be giving birth, but everything will be fine. If you want the drugs, then have them. If you want to give birth on a flying trapeze, that's all right with me. Whatever gets you through. Don't be scared, I'll be there with you, every step of the way."

His words soothed me, that and the distinctive pub logo coming into sight.

"You promise?"

"I promise," he confirmed, as he turned off the ignition.

As we left the car and walked hand-in-hand into the pub his words echoed reassuringly in my ears.

I promise.

CHAPTER 24

Spring sprang, but rain fell daily. Sometimes the raindrops swirled lightly on the air, taking an eternity to land on the already-damp pavement. Then there were the times where the sky turned a heavy leaden grey before dumping bucketfuls of water over the world below.

Getting to work was a challenge on those days, the stream at the end of the road causing flash flooding. I'd suggested catching the metro instead, but Max was having none of it, insisting he could offer a door-to-door taxi service for his pregnant girlfriend. "I've got a responsibility to get you to work safely," he'd replied firmly. "It's not worth taking any risks. I'd never forgive myself if you fell and something happened to you or the baby." It was probably safer to travel on foot than by car, but he was insistent.

When the day we were due to move house rolled around and the weatherman warned of freak storms I feared we might be unable to complete after all. The family we were buying from were relocating to the other end of the country and the whole of the UK had been affected by the weather. Almost everywhere was on amber alert.

Moving from one part of Newcastle to another was one thing, travelling the length of England was another, but when Aliyah, the estate agent I was on first-name terms with, called to say the keys were ready to collect I let out a sigh of relief. Conditions weren't ideal, but after building up to the move, complications and delays would have been devastating. The piles of boxes were becoming claustrophobic and I missed the comfort of my belongings surrounding me. I was definitely ready to start creating our family home.

"You're not lifting a finger," Max ordered, and for once I didn't argue. The house we were moving into might be big, but we were officially combining our lives, and the belongings we'd collected in our collective sixty-three years. We'd accumulated a lot, so I was happy to leave the heavy lifting to Max, the removal men and my dad who'd come along to lend a hand.

The weather remained bone-chillingly cold so my first job was to unpack the kettle and mugs.

"I can barely feel my fingers!" Dad quipped, wrapping both hands around the mug of steaming hot tea, made exactly how he liked it (heavy on the milk, with two sugars). "That hits the spot," he said, taking a grateful gulp.

"We're almost done. It's been a quicker job than I expected," the taller of the two removal men said. "Don't get many people who're as hands-on as you. Most of them leave us to it."

"The sooner everything's in, the sooner we can get it how we want it, right?" Max said, smiling at me. There was a weariness in the way his shoulders were sagging, in how he tilted his head from side to side as though to loosen his stiff neck. It was charming.

"Right," I said, smiling back at him.

It was harder to envisage what the space would look like as ours now it was full of all our belongings. When we'd been to look around it had been someone else's home – clean and stylish and attractive, but most definitely not ours. When we'd swung the door open after turning the key in the lock for the first time, having to jiggle the lock in an unfamiliar way to enter our new home, the blank canvas had seemed full of opportunities.

There were signs of the previous occupants – picture hooks left in the walls, a small splodge of what looked like tomato sauce on the otherwise spotless work surface, the blue water in the loo from where they must have used those weird toilet blocks – but the rooms looked enormous in all their empty glory. Four hours later and all our worldly goods were filling the space. Boxes, bags, suitcases, plus our furniture (in the right rooms, but not the right places) encroached on the space until everywhere looked chaotically messy.

"There's just the chest of drawers, a desk and a small bookcase left," said the shorter of the two removal men to the taller one, rubbing his gloved hands together for warmth. "The sky's gone dark again, I reckon we should get moving before the next downpour."

"All right, Ron," said his colleague, putting his mug of tea down with a sigh of dejection. "Let's bring them in."

As Ron headed outside, the taller man muttered, "Slave driver" under his breath.

"It's a gorgeous house," Dad said, casting his eyes around the living room. "Big windows, high ceilings... I bet it'll be nice in here on a summer's day with the light streaming in."

"Summer seems a long way away at the moment," I said, watching the raindrops slide down the other side of the windowpane. So much for the removal men getting finished before the storm took hold.

"Brighter days will be here before we know it," Dad insisted. "And you'll be settled in by then, all three of you."

His words seemed to set the baby off, as she gave two short, sharp kicks which connected with my ribs. If her power and precision were anything to go by I'd put money on her being the next Kelly Smith, representing England at a future world cup.

"I didn't think there was much to do, but some of the paintwork in the upstairs rooms could do with touching up." I'd noticed Max take a chunk off the white gloss from the door frame as he'd struggled to manoeuvre the bed into the front bedroom. "And I know it doesn't need doing, but I'd like the nursery to be recarpeted and painted," I added sheepishly. So much for saving money, in my mind we were doing our own version of *Changing Rooms*, minus Lawrence Llewelyn-Bowen, thankfully.

"Me and your mum were talking about that," Dad said, knocking back the last of his tea and shifting in his seat as he placed the cup on the windowsill. He reached into the breast pocket of his shirt, pulled out a piece of paper and gave it to me.

At first I didn't realise what it was, but as I took in the recognisable shape and the words written across the front with my dad's familiar scribble of a signature in the bottom right hand corner, my mouth went dry.

"You don't have to do this." The cheque was trembling in my hand. "It's too much."

"We want to," Dad said, folding his hand over mine. The reassurance of his touch calmed me, and although I was still quivering on the inside I was able to keep hold of the piece of paper. The piece of paper that was worth two thousand pounds. "Call it a housewarming gift."

"A pot plant is a housewarming gift. A bottle of wine. Not this amount of money." I was shaking my head as I handed Max the cheque.

"We remember what it was like to be starting out." Dad shrugged. "It's hard. Unexpected expenses pop up, there will be things you'll want to do to make this place feel like home. We want you to be able to do it before the baby arrives. Heaven knows you'll have other priorities once she does."

"This is really kind of you, Mr Drew," Max said. "Really kind of you." But the light behind his eyes wasn't sparkling and I was glad of the interruption of the removal men bringing the chest of drawers through. It diffused the atmosphere, which felt suddenly cooler although I wasn't quite sure why.

CHAPTER 25

It wasn't long until the removal men were on their way, followed shortly after by Dad, who'd been twitchily watching from the window as the rain lashed down.

"You could have been more polite to my dad." I didn't look up from the box I was unpacking. "I know it's not as much as your parents gave us, but it's a lot of money for them."

A wave of protectiveness washed over me.

"I was polite," Max replied defensively, placing the handful of books he'd unpacked on the fitted shelf that ran along the alcove. They landed with a dull thud.

"You were civil. You could have been more grateful."

"I said thank you, what more do you want?" He stood and walked to the window. He let out a huff as he looked out at our new front garden through the rain-blurred window.

The tension was getting to me and I was suddenly aware of the pressure building at the front of my forehead, as though my brain was trying to burst free from the cage of my skull. I'd been warned that the hormone surges of pregnancy might bring on more of the dreaded migraines I'd suffered with since my teens. As pregnancies went, mine had been

143

straightforward. Iris had mentioned sharp pains in her groin which had caused her to writhe in agony, but when she'd questioned the midwife she'd been told it was round ligament pain, which was common apparently. Rachel had struggled with hyperemesis so severe she'd had to be admitted to hospital and put on a saline drip to stop becoming dehydrated, which made my week-long puke-fest sound incredibly tame. Mia had suffered from SPD causing her to struggle to move. So far I'd got off lightly, but the sensations were impossible to ignore.

Max, probably surprised by my lack of comeback, turned around as I sank down into the armchair that had formerly lived in my small box-like house. It had barely been sat in, the couch always being my seat of choice.

"Sophie?" His voice sounded distant, muffled, and bright lights shot in front of my eyes. "Sophie? What's wrong?"

"Migraine," I managed, screwing my eyes tightly shut. I just wanted the light to go away, and the pain.

"Let me help you lie on the settee," he said, and although I was reluctant to move I knew it was the right thing to do. Remaining upright was too much effort, and I somehow knew this would pass more quickly if I were horizontal. "Come on." His voice was soft, the earlier harshness vanishing.

Cautiously I moved my whale-like body, keeping a firm grip on Max's arm as another zigzagged flash of light sliced through me.

"I'd help you up to bed but it's not made yet," he said as I rested my head against a cushion. "You'd hate that."

I could hear the fond teasing in his voice, because he was right. I did like my bedclothes to be just so.

I laid against the fabric of the cushion, aware of the grid-like imprint that the weave was leaving on my cheek, and turned to face the back of the sofa. I could have sworn what little light there was in the room was finding its way through my eyelids, even when they were as tightly closed as humanly possible.

The weight of a blanket fell over me and Max tucked it around my body. My nose tickled, so I buried myself, like a mole digging its way deeper and deeper underground, until I was confident my head was covered and no light could disturb me.

Concentrating on my breathing, the "in-for-five, out-for-five", I'd been practising on and off for years through my YouTube yoga guru Leo, I began to relax. My head still felt as though it might explode, but this was nothing new for me. Migraines were an inconvenient but ever-present part of my life, waiting in the wings for an inopportune moment to strike.

I had no idea of how long I lay there. Max was tiptoeing around in that way that people do where they're trying so hard to be completely silent that they make more noise than they ever would if they were moving naturally.

I stayed on the settee, wrapped up like a burrito, until my head stopped pounding. Slowly emerging from the safety of my bubble I pulled down the "blanket" – only now my vision was clearer and my mind less hazy did I realise it wasn't a blanket at all, it was my coat, a thickly padded khaki maternity coat that Rachel had given me as she no longer needed it. 'It's silly to pay out for one when I've got one that's barely been worn,' she'd said, encouraging me to accept the hand-me-down.

The fake fur trim around the hood grazed my nose and I realised that must have been what I'd felt tickling me earlier. I pushed it away.

"You're awake," Max said gently as I pulled myself up into a sitting position.

"I wasn't sleeping."

"You dozed off for a while, you were snoring."

"I don't snore!"

He looked up from behind the TV stand. "You were snoring

the other night." I knew he was probably right. Breathing had become more challenging since my bump had increased in size, the pressure on my internal organs making every gasp more laboured. "It's nothing to be ashamed of. If anything, it's quite cute."

I rolled my eyes. "Thanks."

"How are you feeling?" he asked, clambering out from his hidey-hole.

"Tired. I'm zapped of energy."

"That's understandable. I've found it tough today with everything going on and it must be ten times harder for you."

"I'm pregnant, not incapacitated."

"Exactly, you're pregnant. That's our baby you're carrying around, that you're keeping warm and fed and healthy and you're doing great. I'd share the load if I could."

"Not long to go and then you can," I said with a smile.

He caught my eye. He was wearing a serious expression.

"I'm sorry I didn't come across as more grateful when your dad gave us the cheque, and I'm sorry if that's one of the things that got you stressed. I'll send him a text and tell him how kind it was for him and your mum to do that for us."

The sincerity was obvious in Max's eyes, but I detected something else too – a glimmer of shame, maybe?

"He'd like that," I said. "They want to help us, Max, and that money will come in really handy. Even if we don't spend it all on renovations it can go towards the baby or bills. I know you say we'll manage the mortgage, but we don't know how much everything else will cost yet either. Heating this place is going to cost double what it did to heat my old house."

That had been a big advantage of the square new-build house I'd rented – it hadn't been much to look at, but it made economic sense. A good location with excellent transport links to the city centre, easy to maintain and cheap to keep warm.

"Speaking of heat, do you want me to have a go at starting the wood burner?" he asked.

He looked like a little kid on scout camp as he placed the wood the previous owners had left behind in the stove and carefully lit it. The amber glow of the flames caused me to squint, but the room immediately felt warmer.

"This is nice," I said, nuzzling my head against his chest as he sat beside me, proudly watching the product of his efforts. "I like watching the flames."

"Me too. It's relaxing." He didn't tear his eyes away from the flickering glow, hypnotised by the dance of the flame. "It's been one hell of a day. The rain's still belting it down."

"I hope my dad got home alright. The roads must be carnage."

"More likely it'll be at a standstill. He'll be fine, he's a careful driver. But you should call if you're worried. I don't want you getting stressed and having another migraine."

I reached for my phone, which was balancing precariously on the arm of the settee, relieved to see there was a text from my dad.

Home safely and Mum's got tea on the table. Fish pie.
Enjoy your first night in your new home. Stay warm. Love you. X

My heart soared as I hurriedly typed back my reply.

Xxx Fire burning so lovely and cosy. Thank you for today. Love you too. Xxx

"Everything okay?"

"He's home," I confirmed. "He'd sent a message earlier telling me he's about to get stuck into a helping of Mum's fish pie."

"Lucky man." Max grinned. "But not as lucky as me. Right now I feel like the luckiest man in the whole world."

"Oh shush," I said, batting playfully at his arm. "You don't need to spout lines. We share a mortgage now, you're tied to me. You don't need to turn on the charm."

"I wasn't! I was only speaking the truth. This is everything I ever dreamed of."

I looked around the room, taking in the boxes – some still sealed and others flat-packed and leaning against the wall, the fire, the floor lamp that Max had presumably lit to save my delicate head, instead of exposing it to the glare of the bare bulb hanging from the light fitting on the ceiling, the now-established fire, with the flames growing taller as the wood caught properly. My trousers pinched around my middle, even though they had an elasticated waistband and as I placed my hand on my stomach our daughter wriggled within me, the sensation like a washing machine on a quick wash. And Max, my beautiful Max, with his hair ruffled after a day of manual labour, his hoodie grubby from lugging boxes.

It was everything I'd ever dreamed of too. Everything I ever dreamed of, and more.

e'd made a pact to have the living room as organised as possible before bedtime so when we came downstairs the next morning we'd have one room already set up, and slowly but surely the room was taking shape. The shelves were full of items from our pasts – photographs and knickknacks, CDs and DVDs – items which were living alongside each other for the very first time. Seeing them together felt momentous, every aspect of our lives colliding.

Each box that we emptied and dismantled was a relief, one step closer to our much-needed bedtime. Not only had it been a long day, but our plan to go to the local chip shop for a celebratory takeaway tea had been scuppered by the Tyne bursting its banks and causing chaos, so instead we'd been running on the cup-a-soups I'd fortuitously packed in the same box as the kettle and half a packet of Hobnobs that the removal men had left behind.

"How many more?" I asked, unable to disguise my weariness. I might have had a snooze earlier on, but the day's events had caught up with me. Migraines always wiped me out.

"Five more boxes of books and then we're done. Oh, and whatever's in the white one in the corner."

My face crumpled into a frown. All the boxes were the same, tan cubes that we'd got from a storage specialist that had been recommended by Mia. There were no white boxes, or at least, there shouldn't have been.

"I thought that was yours."

"Nope, I didn't have any except the ones we bought. All my stuff was in those and the grey suitcase. Except the towels and bedding in those black sacks."

An uncomfortable feeling rippled through me as I edged towards the box. If neither Max nor I had packed it, then who had?

There was a sticky label, printed with my name and the address of our new home, along with a sticker with a logo I immediately recognised. It was the logo for Jessie's mum's shop.

I hadn't changed the address on the wish list, the superstitious side of me not wanting to take any chances in case the sale fell through at the last minute.

So how on earth had a parcel with my name on got here? I had a nasty feeling that even if I opened it, I'd be no closer to getting answers.

CHAPTER 27

"I don't want to open it." Panic was eating me up from the inside, so much so that even looking at the box was making me anxious. "We could take it to the post office and return to sender."

"Except we don't know who that is," Max said, twisting the box around to check. "It's got a postcode for where it was sent from, but I doubt it'll be the sender's. Unless they've written a letter to go with it we'll be no closer to finding out who's sending this stuff."

I could tell he was rankled from the tone in his voice, and even though he was trying to hide it from me, probably because I was a nervous wreck myself when it came to these mystery gifts, he wasn't doing a very good job.

We both eyed the box suspiciously. It was as though now we were aware of its presence we weren't going to be able to think of anything else until we knew what it held. It was goading us, taunting us with its very existence.

"Let's see what's inside."

I waited for Max to take the lead, to pull back the thick

brown tape that sealed the box, but instead he pushed the box across to me, the sound of the cardboard sliding along the polished wooden floor setting my teeth on edge.

Taking a deep breath, I fumbled for the end of the tape, using the tip of my nail to scrape the adhesive from the box. A corner loosened and I pulled the tape off in one long strip. It was almost a flourish.

Max bent over to get a better look as I tentatively peeled back first one flap and then the other to reveal a mass of shredded paper. Pulling it apart and digging into the depths of the box my hands met with something soft and furry. Although I'd only touched it once previously, I knew what it was before I laid eyes on it. The snowsuit from Iris's mother-in-law's shop. As my fingers skimmed the bear ears that were sewn on to the hood I knew for sure.

"So?" Max looked at me impatiently. I'd forgotten that he was none the wiser, that his fingers weren't feeling what I was, and that even if they were he wouldn't know what was inside. He'd had no part in making the wish list.

"I know what it is. It's an outfit I liked in the baby shop."

My heart leapt in my chest as I pulled the item out of the box. It was just as gorgeous as I remembered, from the incomprehensibly tiny foot holes, which were surely too small for an actual human being, even a baby, to fit into to the teddy-bear soft hood.

"There's nothing else?" he said, pulling out the packaging in desperate search for anything that might give a clue to the sender.

"Not that I can see."

I placed the outfit on the settee, my head throbbing again. It was the last thing I needed after the day I'd had.

"I'm going to go to the shop myself and ask some questions.

Surely they can't let just anyone buy something off a gift list? Didn't you have those cards with a code on?"

I'd forgotten about them; lemon-yellow business cards with a hand-written six-digit code so that Iris's mother-in-law could pull up the list of items I'd coveted for any potential gift-buyers. I'd joked at the time that I might give them out to anyone on the street who looked like they had cash to throw around, to see if they'd buy anything for me. I'd never actually expected to receive gifts from someone I didn't know.

"Yes," I managed finally. "And only friends and family were given those." That ruled out Darius, who I'd still been harbouring suspicions about being the secretive giver. This kind of gesture was his style, overblown, ostentatious and showy.

"So it's got to be someone we know," Max said, sinking onto his bottom. He sat cross-legged, like a primary school child on a carpet at story time. "But why would they not tell us if they're buying all these things?"

"Because they don't want to be found out?" I snapped, the pulsing in my head worsening.

"But why?" Max pressed.

"I don't know!" I was all but shouting. "And I don't want to talk about it now. This is supposed to be a special milestone, the first night in our new home. All we've done so far is fight."

I didn't want to give in to the tears that were forcing themselves from behind my eyes, but I couldn't help myself, once the first solitary tear made its break for freedom I was gone, full-on sobbing.

"Hey, hey." Max's arm was around me. "I'm sorry, I shouldn't have kept asking questions when you don't know any more than I do. I hate seeing you cry."

"I don't understand it. If people who love us are sending us things I wish they'd just tell us. It doesn't make any sense."

"It freaks me out too, if I'm honest, but I'm clinging on to the thought that it's someone doing it for the right reasons. They probably think it's nice for us to get gifts when we're not expecting it."

Trust Max to be seeing the good in people rather than being suspicious. It was one of the things I loved about him, but sometimes it annoyed me that he was so damn nice all the time. Times like this for example.

"I'm going to have to ask everyone again. It's eating away at me, even if it is meant as a nice gesture. Who do you think it's most likely to be?"

Max shrugged. "If it was just one item then I'd say it could be anyone, but with it being so many I'd say it's family. Your parents or mine?"

I shook my head. "I don't think so, especially as they've been so generous helping us out with the house."

"One of our siblings then?"

"Maybe." I thought of my sister and her husband in Austria, unless they'd been phoning the shop that seemed unlikely. The baby shop was only small, it didn't have an online outlet. "Nick and Chantel, perhaps? Although I still get the feeling Chantel's not happy that we're going to have the youngest grandchild."

"Or one of my brothers. Not Dale though, he's never got two pennies to rub together and buying baby gifts wouldn't even cross his mind."

I smiled at the thought of Max's youngest brother. Twenty-two and straight out of university, Dale was struggling to find a job that his degree in geology had prepared him for. He was the embodiment of the twenty-something barista dreaming of something more.

"We'll ask them tomorrow at the family get-together."

"If we're not flooded," I joked. "Look at it out there! It's still coming down." Without so much as makeshift curtains covering the windows, the storm beyond the panes of glass made me doubt we'd be able to make it to Max's parents.

The firewood smouldered in the background, the room warming. But I couldn't shake off the uneasy chill I got every time I thought of the gifts. Knowing it was someone we knew should have been reassuring, but it wasn't reassuring at all.

CHAPTER 28

The weather remained typically British – unpredictable. When Max pulled back the spare bedsheet we'd flung over the curtain rail in the bedroom to block out the bright glare of the previous night's lightning (after a much-needed and well-deserved lie-in) we'd expected to be met by a stream flowing down the green. What had faced us was the opposite end of the weather spectrum, powder-blue sky and brilliant sunshine. The trip to Andrea and Hector's was on, and hopefully we'd get closure on the mysterious packages.

"Don't rush," Max instructed, as I stepped out onto the driveway. I'd never lived in a house with a driveway before. "The ground's still slippy. You've got precious cargo on board, don't forget."

Max hadn't been kidding. Despite selecting my flattest, most sensible boots it was a challenge to stay upright on the cobble drive. Yet another case of my centre of gravity shifting throughout pregnancy. My body no longer felt like my own, at least, not the pre-pregnancy body I'd recently begun to accept as "not exactly banging, but all right for a woman in her thirties". It *wasn't* my own, it was my unborn child's home, the blood pulsing through my veins keeping the pair of us alive. Wherever I went, she went, whatever I did impacted on her too. Struck by the enormity of that realisation, I penguin-waddled to the car, happy when my hand connected with the door handle.

"Coo-eee!"

A woman with a tight perm and a gigantic smile waved frantically at me from the other side of the road. I'd guess she was around the same age as my mum, but she looked older – her hair greying around the temples where my mum wasn't ready to say au revoir to the hair dyes that covered the salt and pepper flecks that stubbornly fought back against her styling regime.

Holding tightly to the car with one hand, I gave a small wave to the lady. That was all the encouragement she needed to make her way across the road to strike up a conversation. Although the rain had stopped I wasn't sure the slippers she was wearing were up to the job and I watched on with bated breath, fearful of any slippy patches that lay in waiting to catch her unawares. Relief surged through me when she made it across unscathed.

"Hello, pet. You must be our new neighbours. I'm Julie from number thirty-two." She pointed to a house across the green; identical to ours but for aubergine-coloured woodwork rather than the red of ours that trimmed the window frames. "I was planning to pop round with a plate of home-made biscuits yesterday, nothing much, just a welcoming gift to make you feel at home in our neighbourhood, but the rain came out of nowhere and I didn't get around to it." She smiled apologetically. "So I'll owe you and your husband some biscuits."

"We're not married," I blurted. "Max is my boyfriend."

My hand instinctively clenched against the cold metal of the door handle. I was annoyed with myself for sounding defensive, because it made it seem as though there was something wrong with being pregnant outside of marriage, and I didn't think there was. Julie didn't seem to be the old-fashioned type who was bothered by it either, but the fact I'd felt the need to correct her assumption irritated me.

"I'm sorry," she said, and I wasn't sure if she meant she was sorry that she'd jumped to conclusions or sorry that I was up the duff without a ring on my finger, until she added, "I shouldn't have said that. My daughter's got a baby and she's not married either, but even though lots of people have children without being married I still sometimes forget and let my mouth run away with me."

"It's fine, I wasn't offended," I said, even though I had been mildly put out. "We're serious about each other. Obviously." I laughed. "We wouldn't have bought a house together if we weren't."

"And when's it due?" She glanced down at my bump, protruding through my coat.

"End of May. Not too much longer left to go now."

"Well, I love babies, so if you ever need a hand," she said with a wink.

"Thank you."

"Oh, and I don't suppose you'd like to join the working group for the carnival? May Day weekend, we're holding a community day on the green. It's for the kids, really, and a chance to raise money for the hospice. I'm on the committee and we're always on the lookout for volunteers. Although," she said, looking at my stomach, "you might be tied up by then."

"I'm sure we can help out. Max is great with kids."

"Then I know just the job for him," she said, as I opened the car door. "Nice to meet you, and I'll bring you those biscuits round soon."

"Nice to meet you too. And as for the biscuits, there's really no need."

"Don't be silly," she said, poo-pooing me. "There's always need for biscuits."

I smiled and held my tongue. Who was I to argue with such wisdom from an elder?

"New friend?" Max teased as he joined me, Julie giving another cheery wave as Max and I drove down the road.

"Don't poke fun, she's bringing us home-made biscuits."

"I wasn't making fun. It's nice to meet the neighbours. Perhaps we should have a party once we've got everything organised in the house, it'd be a good way to get to know everyone."

"Well, seeing as I've volunteered you for the carnival working group I think you'll be getting to know them soon enough, but just because they're neighbours doesn't mean we need to live in each other's pockets," I said warily.

In my old house I'd been on nodding terms with my neighbours but that was as far as it went. Oh, there was the one time I'd fed their cat for a week when they were holidaying in Menorca too. I never thought I'd miss that pest of a feline – a ginger tom called Albie, but who I always called Scrat Cat because he was such a scraggly thing – but thinking about him made me miss him, in a strange way.

"But we do have to get on with them. We might be sharing a street with these people for the next ten or twenty years, houses in this neighbourhood don't come onto the market that often."

We rounded the corner onto Max's parents' road, the driving conditions more difficult where the water hadn't had chance to drain away.

"I know, we're lucky."

Max drove onto the driveway, coming to a halt behind his mum's Renault.

"How are we going to bring up the presents?" I asked tentatively. "We've already asked them once and they all denied any knowledge. I don't want to annoy them."

"I'll ask them outright." Max shrugged. "Tell them a gift

arrived at the new house and that it has to be someone who knows about both the gift list and our new address. That doesn't leave many options, we haven't posted out the change of address cards yet."

There was no need because we'd organised for our mail to be redirected. With so much else going on, getting the cards we'd had printed with a photo of the two of us and the address of our new abode to the postbox was low on our list of priorities.

"I hope it is one of them. My brain won't switch off from wondering why whoever it is that's sending them is so keen to keep it secret. It gives me the creeps."

Max reached out and placed his hand on mine before giving a gentle squeeze of reassurance. "If it is we'll know soon enough."

"And if it's not?"

He sighed. "And if it's not, we'll just have to keep asking people until we find out who it is."

Before it even happened I could sense disaster; smell it on the air, taste its bitterness on my tongue. My tiny steps, wary and cautious, got me safely as far as the two steps leading up to Andrea and Hector's house.

But it was the step that defeated me, one stone slab.

My foot skidded, my body connecting with the cold, hard ground. Despite the shock I somehow managed to manoeuvre my body so I landed on my back rather than my front, my coccyx slamming forcibly against the hard surface.

I yelped as pain shot up my spine. Max rushed to my aid, but even having him there wasn't enough to calm me.

Breathing was impossible, I was gulping at the air, inhaling what little traces of breath I was exhaling before it could escape into the atmosphere. It reminded me of when I'd fainted at Tawna's wedding in what we now knew were the very early weeks of pregnancy, long before we even thought of taking a test.

The fear ballooned inside me, pressing against my skin. I couldn't decide whether or not blacking out entirely was better, at least then I wouldn't have the barrage of thoughts of the worst kind taking over my brain.

What if I've damaged the baby?

Shit, the baby's not moving. What if I've killed the baby?

What if the baby is fine but I've caused irreversible damage to my spinal cord?

Every negative outcome flashed against the backs of my closed eyes.

"Sophie? Soph?"

Max put his hand on my shoulder and where his touch usually reassured me, instead I was met by another jolt of pain charging through me.

"It hurts so much." My voice was halfway between a whine and whiney. "I'm scared to move."

Andrea opened the door, presumably alerted of our arrival by the commotion, and at the sight of her I started to cry. What is it about being sick or injured that makes me long for my own mum with all my heart and soul? Max's mum is lovely – kind, gentle, genuinely brimming over with compassion – but she's not my own mum. Andrea never brought me hot Ribena when I was feeling under the weather, never tucked my favourite pink fleecy blanket around me, never placed a pile of trashy magazines in front of me with a tut and a smile when I had a raging temperature.

"Oh, Sophie! What are you doing down there?"

"I skidded on the step," I said evenly, although it didn't require an answer. The question was rhetorical.

"Give me your arm, come on," she said, hooking her arm through mine. "Max, you take her other arm," she instructed, looking at her son, "and take your time, Sophie. There's no rush. Although you must be freezing down there, your jeans are soaked."

Slowly but surely I placed the flats of my feet on the ground. With Max supporting one side of me and Andrea the other I tentatively allowed them to guide me from the floor to standing.

"That's it," she soothed, as I managed to step into the hallway. "Easy does it."

Shock was still rippling through me, along with fear, and tears continued to fall, tears of panic. I'd never forgive myself if something had happened to the baby.

"It's okay, Soph." Max rubbed the base of my spine and I winced. I wondered if the skin was grazed, because it felt as though my tailbone had been attacked by a madman with a cheese grater. "Don't panic. You're safe now."

"I'm scared. What if... what if I've hurt the baby?" Even saying the words aloud made my stomach writhe. Then, in a voice so small I could barely hear it myself, I added, "I can't feel her moving."

"That's not unusual though, is it?" Max replied, far more calmly than I expected. True, he usually was the more rational of the two of us and whereas I had been known to thrive off drama, Max liked a steady, quiet life. "You can't feel her move all the time."

"I don't feel right. I want to go to the hospital, just to make sure."

"Now?"

"Yes, Max, now! What if there's something wrong?"

Andrea, who had disappeared into the large oak-panelled kitchen reappeared, a pint glass of Coke in her hand. She offered it to me and I noticed the ice cubes bobbing on top of the brown liquid like miniature glaciers.

"I don't want a drink," I said, my stomach churning anxiously. How could she expect me to chug a pint of pop when I was worried sick?

"Try it." She handed me the glass.

The chill of it against my hands almost burned.

I took a sip, the bubbles tingling against my throat as I swallowed.

"That's the way," she said with a smile. "Keep going." She nodded her encouragement.

"I really don't feel like it–"

"Trust me," she interrupted. "Works like a charm every time. This one was a real little bugger for scaring us silly," she said, looking pointedly at Max. "He was the least wriggly of the lot. Laid back from the off, that's what Hector always says, but whenever I drank this stuff the sugar rush must have gone to his head as he'd start kicking away like Bobby Charlton. The colder the better too, that's why I put the ice cubes in."

"How... how did you know I was worried?"

She smiled softly. "You're a pregnant woman who's had a fall. It's only natural you're going to be concerned but if we try the Coke trick hopefully it'll be enough to get this little princess moving and putting her mummy and daddy at ease."

I took a large gulp of the Coke, the ice cubes bashing against my front teeth, and hoped Andrea was right. I'd feel happier once I felt that familiar twisting in my stomach, the weird sensation that made me feel as though my womb was a tumble drier and our daughter a bedsheet tying itself in knots.

Nothing.

"It's not working, nothing's happening." I was aware I sounded borderline hysterical, but I couldn't be rational, not when I was so scared. "Will you take me to the hospital, Max, please?"

I was acutely aware of the throbbing across my buttocks and lower back but all of that paled into insignificance compared to my racing heart, pounding against the darkest thoughts I just couldn't shake.

"Of course," he said, wrapping an arm around my waist. His fingers caressed the curve of my hipbone, skimming so his fingertips rested against the outer edges of my stomach.

That was the very moment our daughter chose to start squirming with such ferocity that I wondered what she was doing in there. The hokey cokey? The Macarena? Whatever cheesy dance it was, I didn't care, I was overcome with relief.

"Can you feel it?" I asked with a laugh I couldn't hold back.

"I feel it," Max said, pulling me into a hug. "That's our daughter's way of reassuring us."

The wriggling continued, joy washing over the pair of us that our worst fears were unwarranted.

"I still think we should go to the hospital, just in case. They might be able to do a scan."

"I'm not risking you walking down that step again," Max said protectively. "Let's go out of the back door. Although there's a drop down, the path is less slippery."

"My hero." I grinned.

We walked through the kitchen, where the Oakley rabble were gathered, chatting noisily in small groups. The atmosphere was warm, the air laced with good-natured teasing and laughter, and I wished that we could stay. Not only were my relationships with Max's brothers and their families growing with each week we spent together, I felt as though they'd taken me under their wings and allowed me into their fold. In fact, all three of them had individually told me how pleased they were that their brother had finally fallen in love and was settling down. "Just

Dale to sort out now, and I think that one might take a while," Grant had teased affectionately.

"We're not stopping," Max said, as his nephew, Dylan, ran over at full pace. "We're heading out the back way because it's less slippery than the drive."

"You'll come back when you're done, won't you?" Andrea said, looking mildly concerned. "There's masses of curry and enough rice to feed an army."

"As long as we're not waiting too long to be seen then we'll be back," Max promised. "Save me a big helping."

"I will, don't you worry," his mum said with a smile. "Like I said there's far too much anyway. I put in all the potatoes I had. Even Grant wouldn't be able to make his way through this lot, and you know what his appetite's like."

Max snorted with laughter as Grant sucked in his stomach. That didn't stop him ladling more of the curry onto his plate.

"Drive safely." Chris slapped his brother on the back as Max pulled open the French doors.

"I'm sure everything's fine, but it's worth getting Sophie and the baby checked over. Can't be too careful when it comes to my girls."

Hearing him refer to me and the baby as his girls made my heart balloon.

"Too right," Chris replied. "Hope it goes well and you get seen quickly."

"Cheers, bro."

Max took my hand and led me over the threshold and into the garden. "Promise you won't move a muscle." He peered at me over the upper rim of his glasses like a schoolteacher chiding a naughty child.

"I promise," I replied mock-meekly. I wasn't going to take any chances. Admittedly, I was feeling less stiff since I'd massaged the sore spot that had connected with the ground, but the panic

I'd felt when I worried I'd seriously damaged my child was enough to make me listen. I wasn't going any further until Max parked the car right next to me.

He leant down and kissed the top of my head, his upper lip tangling in my hair. "Good. I love you so much, Sophie Drew."

"I love you too."

In all the excitement I'd forgotten about the packages.

"Do you feel happier now?" he asked and I nodded. "Definitely."

The triage nurse had done all the usual observations – checking my blood pressure, listening for Baby's heartbeat – but agreed that given the circumstances it would be worth scanning me to ensure there was no internal damage.

The words had set my worst nightmares into action again, fears that even if the baby was fine I could have damaged my womb or the placenta or something. Eve was right, pregnancy was a miracle, but there were so many elements that had the potential to go wrong.

The sonographer – a different woman to the one who'd done our previous scans, who was more adept at ensuring the gel stayed on the area being scanned rather than on my clothes – had been quick to tell us that this was precautionary, and not to worry if she was quiet as she had a look at what was going on inside my womb. We were old-hands now, we knew the drill.

"One happy, healthy baby." She grinned and turned the monitor to face us. "It was worth coming in though, especially if you were worried."

"Worried sick," Max confirmed as she handed me a paper towel to wipe the slimy gel from my stomach.

"In situations like this it's always better to come in. Babies are well protected in there, but it's better to be sure."

"Thank you so much," I gushed.

"You take care out there," she said, before pressing a grainy scan photo into the palm of my hand.

"Oh, I've not got any money on me," I said.

Buying a photo had been the last thing on my mind, all I'd wanted was assurance everything was okay.

"Call it a gift." She brought her finger to her lips. "Just don't tell anyone out there or they'll all be wanting one." She nodded towards the waiting area.

"My lips are sealed." I mimed drawing a zip closed. "We won't tell a soul."

"Thank you," Max said, holding out his hand in an offer of a handshake. "You've been fantastic."

"It's just my job," she said.

I shook my head. "You've gone over and above."

"Have a lovely evening now, and I prescribe putting your feet up and doing as little as possible," she said as she held the door open for us to leave the ultrasound room. "Everything's fine, but that doesn't mean you need to try and win any marathons."

"No fear of that," I said with a grateful smile.

As Max and I made our way back to the car we talked about how we wouldn't see our baby again until we properly met her. No more scans (although I had been tempted by a private 4D scan after reading online reviews of how wonderfully clear they were). There were just four weeks to go until due date, and although I wasn't naïve enough to expect Baby to pop out on the day that we'd been counting down to, especially since I'd seen that only around four per cent of babies arrived on their actual due date, there was a red circle on the calendar.

"We really need to start thinking seriously about a name," Max said as he pulled out of the car park and onto the main road. Traffic was slow, despite it being a weekend. It always was around the hospital.

"You like really weird names though." I wrinkled up my nose.

"They're not weird, they're traditional," Max countered.

"Old-fashioned."

"Classic."

"I don't want to call my daughter Prudence." I rolled my eyes. "There's got to be something we can agree on."

"How about we go through the baby name book again together and make a list of any names we both like."

"That sounds like a plan."

I relaxed back into the seat, being careful to leave a gap between the grazed base of my back and the faux leather seat. That was no mean feat with the seat belt strap determined to restrain me.

I caught sight of Max stealing a glance at the dashboard clock. "Are we going back to my parents or would you rather head home and put your feet up?"

Part of me longed to get home and do nothing for the remainder of the day, but I also wanted to catch up with Max's family. There were questions that remained unanswered that would be easier to pose in person rather than by phone or WhatsApp.

"Don't let me be the one to keep you from your mum's curry." I smiled. "I know how much you love it."

"There will be plenty of other opportunities to eat my mum's curry. I understand if you'd rather be in our own home."

I didn't have the heart to say that as lovely as the new house was it hadn't reached the magical "home" status yet. In total we'd spent a maximum of twenty-four hours there and an abundance of boxes took over every room but the lounge.

"Let's go back to your parents. You were going to ask about the delivery, remember?"

I hoped Max would take the lead on the conversation. His family would probably think I was completely off my head, either hormonal or delusional.

"I'll ask them," he replied, "but I really don't think any of them are behind it. Are you sure it's not your family?"

"I sent Anna another message and it's not her. Nick hasn't replied yet, but I'd be surprised if it was him and Chantel. They've got enough on with Noah and the twins, they haven't got time to chase around buying random gifts. I'll talk to Mum and Dad about it tomorrow, but it's not them, I know it. They'd have just given us a present if they'd wanted to, they wouldn't have got them delivered without even telling me about it."

Despite everything I still couldn't shake the feeling that Darius was somehow behind the deliveries. He might not have the code to access my wish list, but he was best friends with Johnny and could have seen the little card with the details on pinned on their kitchen noticeboard. I'd also given Nadia a card when I'd invited her to the baby shower Tawna and Eve were organising, so he could have seen it when he was collecting Summer. It wouldn't take much for him to snap a photo on his phone and then take matters into his own hands. I wouldn't put anything past him.

"I'll ask my family," Max promised. "But I'll choose my moment carefully. If it is one of them I don't want them to think we're not grateful."

"But make it clear how freaked out it made us," I persisted. "Even if it is done with good intentions the whole thing has a sinister edge."

"You've been watching too many horror films."

"You know I prefer a romcom. I don't think I've seen a horror film since *The Blair Witch Project* when I was fifteen. It freaked me and Eve out so badly that I made the decision I wasn't going to watch anything scary again."

"You're just a softie," he said gently. He took his eyes off the road briefly and as they connected with mine a ripple of love surged through me. "It's one of the things I love about you."

"One of the things?"

"Stop fishing for compliments," he said wryly, his eyes firmly back on the road as we drove onto the outer edges of his parents' suburban estate. "You know I love you."

"I do, but it's still nice to hear it," I said with a mock-pout.

"I love the way you sing the wrong words to old songs. I love the way you bite down on your lip when you're nervous. I love how you eat cupcakes, licking off every bit of buttercream before biting into the cake. I love that you're loyal, and funny, and kind. Is that enough compliments for you to be going on with?"

"Is that it?" I said, pretending to be irritated. "Surely there's more than that that you love about me."

A smirk crossed his face as he pulled back onto the driveway in front of his parents' house.

"There is one other thing." I waited expectantly, when his eyes twinkled mischievously before looking down at where my more-humongous-than-ever chest was squashed into a maternity bra that was clearly not big enough.

"My boobs?!" I laughed.

"Well they are pretty fantastic," he said as he unclipped his seat belt. "Especially now."

"I don't know what to say. You've left me speechless."

"There's a first time for everything." He winked and I swatted his arm.

As he climbed out of the car, the vehicle shaking as he slammed the door behind him, I could still hear him chuckling to himself, but when he came and opened the passenger side door to accompany me safely back into the house he leant over and kissed my lips.

"It wasn't just your boobs," he whispered, "although they are majestic. It was everything."

CHAPTER 30

Two stupidly large bowls of curry and one bout of indigestion later (what is it with pregnancy and heartburn?) I was still waiting for Max to broach the subject of the unexplained packages with his family. In fact, I think the stress of waiting for him to spit it out made my digestive problems worse.

He'd left it so long to say anything that Grant and Belinda were getting ready to leave. That was the point where I had to take matters into my own hands.

"Max." I prodded him in the ribs with my finger, hard enough for him to squirm. "Wasn't there something you were going to ask?"

I threw him a withering look as he shifted awkwardly on the spot.

"Err... yeah."

Grant pulled on a baseball cap emblazoned with the badge of the local cricket team. They should have been playing but waterlogged pitches had put paid to almost all the fixtures nationwide, and the north east, as so often, was one of the worst-hit areas.

"What's up, bro?" Grant asked, a teasing affection in his tone. "If it's a loan you're after, you still owe me a pint from the other week."

"It's not a loan. I – we – just wanted to make sure that it wasn't you who'd bought us baby clothes to be delivered to the new house."

The puzzled look on both of their faces was all the answer I needed.

"Nope. We were waiting until baby arrived before we bought anything," Grant said.

"Except for something small that I couldn't resist buying to bring to the baby shower," Belinda added sheepishly. "Those little outfits are so cute."

A sigh of frustration escaped my lips. It was only after I'd huffed that I realised it sounded like I was ungrateful that Belinda had bought baby clothes.

The hurt was evident in the straight-line her lips formed, in the narrowing of her eyes.

"I'm sorry," I said, "I wasn't sighing at you, I promise. I bet whatever you've chosen is adorable, you've got great taste."

That brought a tentative smile back onto her face, and I wasn't trying to flatter her, she really did have excellent taste. As an interior designer she had an eye for colour and pattern, and Isaac always looked stylishly dressed for a child his age.

"It's just getting to us that someone's sending presents and not saying who they're from," Max explained.

"I think it's nice," Grant said with a shrug. "I love surprises."

"I don't." I shuddered, remembering the "surprise" party Eve and Tawna had thrown to celebrate me reaching thirty. "I like to know what's coming so I can prepare. That's why I'd never have been able to have been one of those people who didn't find out the gender until the birth."

"I'll bear that in mind for future reference," Belinda said.

"No surprises for Sophie. But no, the deliveries are nothing to do with us. Sorry."

I smiled weakly. "We'll ask Chris. Maybe he knows something about it."

The rest of the family filed through to wave them off, before we all reassembled in the kitchen. I deliberately positioned myself near Chris, feigning interest in the conversation he was having with Hector about jump leads.

"Chris," I started, "I know I asked you about this a while ago, but you don't know anything about these deliveries we've been getting from our baby gift list, do you?"

He shook his head. "You've had more of those weird deliveries without a message?"

I nodded, relieved that he was seeing it my way. After Grant's diffidence I'd begun to wonder if I really was overreacting.

"There must have been a package waiting for us when we arrived at the house yesterday because when we were unpacking all the boxes for the lounge there was another one."

"That's weird."

"Tell me about it. I just want to know who's sending them now. The stuff they've given us isn't cheap either. If I was giving elaborate gifts I'd want to make damn sure the person receiving them knew they were from me."

"Exactly. Anyone would." His brows lowered, as I'd noticed often happened when he concentrated. "Unless it's someone really rich."

"That rules out everyone we know," I said with a laugh. Max's family were well off compared to mine, but they didn't throw their money around with wild abandon. And Max's friends were all the poor creative type. His closest friends, Oz, Archie and Iain were in a band who were reaching dizzy heights on the local circuit but barely scraping a living as they travelled around the region in a battered old minivan which carried their instruments, amps and guitar pedals.

The only people we knew that came close to what would qualify as rich were Tawna and Johnny, and I'd already asked Tawna if it was her sending the gifts and she'd categorically denied it. "I'm sure we'll find out who's behind it before long, but I'd feel better about having the stuff in the house if I knew who they were from."

"Yeah, I get that. You don't think it's Darius do you?" Chris said, lowering his voice to a conspiratorial whisper. He knew of my ex because they were in the same line of work. More than once he'd confided that my ex continued to use his charming ways to manipulate people. In the world of business it could be disguised as nous, but in real life, where hearts were on the line, it was far from that. I'd been on the receiving end of his patter many times, swept up in his flattery. I knew better than most what he was like. I'd been oblivious to it at the time, of course. At the time I'd thought he was "the one".

I pulled a face. "It's crossed my mind. I've not seen him in ages, but he must know I'm pregnant. We have too many friends in common for him to have not heard it on the jungle drums."

"Do you want me to ask him? There's a conference for people in the building trade this week and I bet he'll be there. It'd save you having to talk to him."

As appealing as it was to take him up on it, I shook my head. "Thanks, but I think it's something I'm going to have to deal with. I'll text him. He'll probably ignore me, but I'm going to have to woman up and ask him."

"Do it now." He slid my phone across the table towards me. "Don't think about it, just do it."

"I hope I don't regret this..." I clicked on the message icon and started drafting the text. "What if he says he knows nothing about it?"

In a strange way I liked how the anonymity meant I could turn Darius into a scapegoat. Since he'd lied to me, telling me he needed money to keep his daughter closer to him when in truth he was spending it in Vegas on Johnny's stag do, I'd been alerted to his true colours. He might be handsome and he might talk the talk, but he could be a first-class bastard.

"Trust your gut. If you think it's him, it probably is."

My gut had let me down many times in the past when it came to Darius Welch, that was the problem.

That along with not knowing how to start the message. "Hi" sounded too friendly, "Good evening," too formal. To launch straight in felt accusatory, and I didn't want him to put his defences up. Darius was the type of man who responded to his ego being massaged.

In the end I settled on a simple message that I hoped sounded conversational and, in case the gifts were from him, made sure to mention how grateful we were.

Max and I have received some lovely presents from our baby gift list, but some have arrived without a message saying who has kindly given us them. If this might have been you, please let us know so we can say thank you!

I hoped it came across as bright and breezy but that it had the tone of a round robin message.

Within minutes my phone vibrated, rattling against Max's parents' glass-topped dining table.

Congratulations Sophie.I know you always wanted to be a mum. The presents werent from me though.D

I swallowed down the lump that had lodged itself in my throat at his words. I had always wanted to be a mum, and the chance to be a step-mum of sorts to Summer had only hammered home how important it was to me to have a family of my own.

His congratulations shouldn't matter to me, but they did. I wasn't looking for his seal of approval, nor making the point that I'd moved on, but it felt like closure, in a weird way.

The worst part of the message, apart from the appalling punctuation and grammar, was the last line.

The presents werent from me though.

And although he'd lied to me so many times in the past, my gut was convinced that this time Darius was telling the truth, the whole truth and nothing but the truth. But if it wasn't him sending the presents, who was it?

CHAPTER 31

"Carnival weekend next week," Eve mused, as she poured herself a glass of Pinot Grigio. "Funny to think we're almost into May. A third of the year's gone already."

"Don't." Tawna winced. "Time's going too quickly. I'm not ready for another birthday just yet."

"Pah." I waved away her worries with a swish of my hand. "Thirty-one isn't so bad, I promise. But you're right about this year flying by. Next month I'll be a mum!"

I pulled my mouth into a wide, nervous smile. I knew I probably looked like Wallace from the Wallace and Gromit animations, but I couldn't help myself. This was a big deal.

"Less than four weeks left until due date and I'm seriously underprepared."

Tawna looked at me, an incredulous expression on her face. "Underprepared? I've seen your house and it looks ready to me. She's got as many clothes as I have and she's not even been born yet."

"And beautifully arranged too," Eve teased, referring to how I'd organised them by colour, hanging first the neutral shades before arranging the miniature outfits into a rainbow spectrum.

179

"Either you've been scouring Pinterest for ideas or you've stolen them straight from Iris's mum-in-law's shop."

"Oh shush," I said with a smile, secretly thrilled that both my friends had noticed the effort I'd gone to to ensure the room looked like it belonged in the spreads in the glossy catalogues of baby paraphernalia. "And yes, in terms of all the stuff we need we're prepared. It's mentally that we're not quite ready yet."

"I'm not sure it's something anyone's ever ready for," Chantel chipped in from the other side of the island that divided Eve's living area from her kitchen. "When I was expecting Noah I read all the books, watched *One Born Every Minute* religiously and spent hours writing out my birthing plan. It all went out of the window when I was begging for an epidural but that was the first lesson of parenthood. It's all about winging it, and you can plan all you want but things don't always turn out the way you expect them to."

Yet again, Chantel with the negatives. I didn't like the tension between us, but without asking outright if she had a problem with the fact I was pregnant, I didn't know how to fix it. The baby shower wasn't the time nor the place to broach the subject.

"I don't like feeling out of control," I admitted, swiping a cupcake from the counter. The tray of sweet treats had been taunting me ever since I'd arrived for the baby shower and I could no longer resist the thick marshmallow pink icing that topped the spongy delights. Never mind that there were still people to arrive, I was ready to get stuck into the food. "If I wasn't so scared by the thought of surgery I'd have asked about an elective caesarean so I'd know exactly when she was going to arrive."

"She'll arrive when she's meant to," Andrea said wisely, "and you can decide how you feel on the day as to whether or not you want drugs. There's no medals for not having them, you know. Chris was enormous, and got stuck. I was bloody-minded and had it in my head that I shouldn't need any drugs because women had been having babies for millennia without them but it was agony. When I had Max I'd have taken every type of pain relief they offered but in the end I didn't need it. He pretty much fell out, an hour from the first twinge to holding him in my arms. My pelvic floor had been shot to pieces by the time he arrived, thanks to Chris."

"Quick sounds appealing."

"Not always best for baby though," Belinda chipped in. "Birth is traumatic and I'm not just talking about for Mum. Imagine being a baby, all comfortably tucked up in a womb and then whoosh! You're being squeezed down the birth canal head first into a noisy, bright new world. No wonder none of us remember being born, it must be horrific."

Thankfully the buzzing of the intercom interrupted her horror stories, with Iris, Jessie, Mia and Rachel arriving together. It was especially lovely to see Iris and Jessie, and to meet their new daughter, Dana, who was strapped to Jessie's front. It was strange to think they were such new friends. It felt like I'd known them for much longer than a mere few months.

"Hello!" Mia cooed, her head hidden by the enormous nappy cake she was carrying. "Where can I put this? It's heavier than it looks."

Eve guided her towards the dining table, laden with the spread that both my mum and Max's mum had taken charge of. Between the two of them there was enough to feed the five thousand. The group (me, Tawna, Eve, Mum, Andrea, Chantel, Belinda, Jane and Kath from work, Jessie, Iris, Mia and Rachel) would do our best to demolish the buffet, but I didn't fancy our chances. It was almost enough to make me wish I'd invited more people, but I'd asked everyone I'd wanted there, it was just a shame that my boss, Marcie, was visiting family in Cumbria and that Norma was living the life of luxury on a Caribbean cruise. I didn't begrudge her the trip – she'd been struggling to cope since her beloved husband, Fred, died the previous year – but it would have been lovely for her to have been part of the celebrations. Despite her failing eyesight she'd painstakingly been knitting, straining to complete the intricate cable work, and the cardigans she'd given me when I'd popped over to see if she needed anything fetching from the shops were among my favourite items of clothing for the baby. As I'd held them in my hands I could have sworn I could feel the love in each and every stitch.

"Right," said Tawna, clapping her hands together in an authoritarian fashion, "now that everyone's here we can get started." She beamed at the guests, pivoting to meet the gaze of each and every woman in the place as though she was the eye candy on a rerun of an eighties gameshow. Anyone would think it was her baby shower, or at least her flat. "We're going to start with some games, so Eve's going to give you each a pen and paper. The first round is a picture round with photos of famous people when they were babies, so you can start on that straight away, then in five minutes' time I'll be moving on to the music round."

Everyone promptly ignored Tawna's "no conferring" rule as they squinted to try and identify the pudgy-faced tots on the papers they were handed.

"I'm sure I know those eyes," Rachel said, covering up the rest of one of the baby faces with her palm. "Do you think it's Robbie Williams?"

I tilted my head, not convinced. "Maybe."

"Harry Styles?" she suggested. "Or Richard Osman?"

I shrugged, looking at my own answer – Katy Perry. "Your guess is as good as mine."

"What about number three?" Mum asked, peering over at

my answer. "I thought it might be Geri Halliwell because of the red hair, but now I'm wondering if it could be Fergie."

"I'm sure that one's Nicole Kidman," I answered, noticing Rachel furiously scribbling the name down on the dotted line beneath the picture of the toddler. "I've seen it before on a documentary."

"Ooh, I think you're right," Mum said with a nod of approval.

"Two more minutes," Tawna bellowed over our chatter, "we've got a lot to fit in so it's vital we stick to the schedule." I was surprised she wasn't tapping her watch to further drum home her point.

I hurriedly guessed the other answers, not convinced by any of them, before swapping papers with Mia for the marking process.

"It's like being back at school," she whispered from behind a cupped hand. "And everyone laughed at me then too."

I took the liberty of looking at her answers, which were even more outlandish than mine – I highly doubted Tawna would have included pictures of Theresa May as a baby in the quiz – I doubted she even knew who Theresa May was.

"I won't laugh," I promised, crossing my heart with my index finger. "I guessed at most of them myself, and my mum named every red-head in the world before finally getting the Nicole Kidman one," I chuckled.

Mia's eyes widened in horror. "Nicole Kidman? I thought that was Ed Sheeran."

There was no way in the world but I didn't want to make her feel bad so said, "Maybe you're right. We'll find out the answers in a minute."

Tawna proceeded to read out the answers to shouts of "I should have got that one" and frustrated groans. I felt bad when I handed Mia back her answer sheet and she'd only got two of the twelve right.

Her face fell as she looked at her score.

"Tawna's got loads more games planned. Maybe the one where we have to guess which chocolate bar she's melted into a nappy will be better suited to your talents."

"You know me so well. Chocolate is my *Mastermind* specialist subject." Mia laughed as Tawna explained the music round – naming the artist. Thankfully for all of us her choices were pop-heavy and even Mum and Andrea were able to recognise the openings to "Baby One More Time" by Britney Spears and Take That's "Babe".

We giggled our way through a game where everyone cut a piece of string to the length that they thought would fit around my bump (all of them vastly overestimating, which I took to mean I looked particularly heifer-like) and Mia did indeed excel at naming the chocolate bars which filled an array of disposable nappies.

"Just one more game to go before we design baby vests," Tawna said excitedly, "but we'll have to wait to find out the answers on this one. We know Baby Oakley-Drew is going to be a girl, but this is the sweepstake for both the baby's weight and the name Sophie and Max are going to choose. Sophie's been very tight-lipped about the whole thing," Tawna said, her voice light and breezy. "I've tried getting it out of her but with no luck. She's being very mysterious."

I played up to my enigmatic reputation by winking theatrically, but the reality was that I didn't have a clue – Max and I still couldn't agree on a name.

Everyone started discussing possibilities, throwing out suggestions of names from the traditional to the wild and I nodded politely to each and every option, pretending to consider them as a real contender. It was getting to me, not having a name set in stone. I was sure that once we had one it'd be another step closer to feeling like the person within me was a real little human being rather than an abstract bump.

Eve removed the napkins that covered the plates of food, revealing the most delicious-looking nibbles.

My stomach grumbled in anticipation. If I was hungry before, I was suddenly ravenous.

That was when it happened, although I don't know how. The leg of the drop-leaf table must have been knocked as everyone jostled at the thought of food and, as though happening in slow motion, the elaborate nappy cake fell, the carefully tied nappies bouncing off the floor as a cascade of food landed on top of them.

Eve's mouth formed a horrified "o", Rachel's hands coming up to her own mouth to catch the squeak that escaped her lips. Mum moved forward to catch the bowls of food but it was hopeless. Coleslaw and hummus, salsa and Thousand Island dressing splattered not just over the pure-white nappies and vests that made up the "cake" but also over Eve's carpet.

For what felt like a lifetime I stood frozen, not sure how to react, which was when I saw Tawna, tears of frustration in her eyes. I knew she'd see this as a personal failure. She loved being the centre of attention, but only when things were going to plan. Her ability to relinquish control was on a par with mine.

"Kitchen roll!" Tawna ordered, the whites of her eyes fractured by red lines of crazy-paving where she was trying but failing to hide her upset. "There's still plenty of food, so it'll be fine once we've cleared up the mess."

She lowered to her haunches and scrubbed at the carpet. Jessie and I exchanged looks – it was apparent that she was making it worse, but neither one of us was about to approach her. I knew Tawna well enough to see when she was near explosion, like a bottle of fizzy pop that had been shaken, the pressure building against the constraints of the roof, and Jessie had noticed the tense line of her shoulders, the abrupt motion of her arms as she tried with desperation to clear up the mess.

"Is she okay?" Jessie mouthed, cocking her head to the side in her direction.

I shrugged helplessly. The flat was too small to be able to talk to Tawna one on one and she'd hate it if I drew attention to her in this less-than-perfect situation. Tawna was used to life falling in line with her plans.

"There," Tawna said finally stepping back, a fire burning behind her eyes as though to dare anyone to mention the irregularly shaped pinkish stain on the carpet. "Tuck in, everyone."

She beckoned us over, forcing paper plates decorated with pastel coloured nappy pins onto everyone. "Go on, eat up. There's plenty."

The atmosphere had changed, tension rife in the airless flat.

I bided my time, not wanting to pressurise her, but kept a watchful eye over Tawna as she ensured the guests piled their plates high. Once everyone was settled, digging into the food (there was still more than we'd ever manage to eat) I noticed Tawna stealthily pouring herself a large glass of Prosecco and downing it in one, before refilling her glass and knocking that back too. So much for her not drinking, she was necking it like this was her big night out. She turned to face me, painting on a smile before walking to the corridor, presumably to use the bathroom.

I never really enjoyed baby showers when they were for other people, and although the event had been arranged out of love I wasn't having much more fun at my own. My St Clement's "mocktail" didn't help me lose my inhibitions in the same way a gin and tonic would.

I kept a watchful eye on the door, anticipating Tawna returning to the room with a face like thunder. Things always went smoothly for her, maybe her Irish ancestry bringing her luck. She wasn't used to mishaps, she breezed through her charmed life without a care. But I did feel for her. Despite her flaws her heart was in the right place and that she'd gone to all this effort was so very typically Tawna.

When my friend's face appeared, her smile seemed wider than ever, or perhaps that was down to how she had reapplied her lipstick. "Right!" she chirruped. "Where were we?"

The party games continued, with everyone other than me slowly becoming more and more tipsy, which in turn led to some ridiculously wide-off-the-mark guesses in the remaining games.

By the time everyone was waving their goodbyes my body ached all over and I could gladly have fallen into Eve's chair and dozed like a woman three times my age, but Tawna had other ideas.

"Time to open the gifts," she sang, gesturing to the pile of presents in the corner of Eve's living room. Everyone had been so generous, the stack of candyfloss-pink parcels and gift bags was huge.

"Can I have a coffee first?" I begged. "I can barely keep my eyes open."

Tawna tutted. "Didn't you have a coffee when you got here? I thought you were only having one a day because caffeine is bad for the baby."

"I am allowed to have more than one cup a day, you know," I replied, the metaphorical chip on my shoulder evident in my voice. "Compared to what I normally drink I've hardly had any for months. I'm sure it's fine in moderation, when Chantel was pregnant with the twins she regularly had a glass of wine with her meal. Her midwife said it was fine so long as she didn't go overboard."

Tawna's brow furrowed. "Seems like unnecessary risks to me."

Eve turned from filling the hob-top kettle, flicked on the gas and rolled her eyes. "Come on now. Sophie wants a coffee. It's not like she's injecting heroin into her eyeballs."

"Okay, okay," Tawna conceded, throwing up her hands in a dramatic fashion. "It's not like I have any knowledge on the subject anyway."

An awkward silence hung between us until it was broken by the shrill whistle of the kettle reaching boiling point.

"Right," Eve said as she reached three mugs down from the cupboard. "Coffees all round?"

CHAPTER 32

The coffee worked its magic on my short temper and even Tawna's judgey looks weren't enough to get my back up. Caffeine really did work miracles.

"I don't know where to start," I said with a laugh, faced with the mountain of gifts. "Look how much there is!"

Eve nodded. "They do say babies need a lot of stuff."

"Tell me about it. When Nick and Chantel had Noah, their house was full of bouncy chairs and the like. Then the twins came along and it's impossible to move in their house. Chantel mentioned she's had to put her dining chairs in the attic out of the way now there are three of them in high chairs. Mum told me she fell over one the other day."

"Child or high chair?" Eve said, with a grin that showed she knew full well what I meant.

I rolled my eyes at my friend's rubbish joke. "Very funny."

"Was I imagining it or did Chantel seem kind of weird today?" Tawna pulled a face that suggested anyone who came to a baby shower she'd helped arrange and didn't have a whale of a time had problems.

"She's like that all the time lately. I thought I mentioned it before? Me and Max think it's because she'd worried our baby's going to be the favourite and Mum and Dad will forget about Noah and the twins."

"As if!" Eve scoffed.

"I know, it's ridiculous. It's not like we got pregnant just to spite them."

"I'm sure they know that," Tawna said. "Maybe there's more to it than meets the eye. No one knows what goes on behind closed doors."

I let out a laugh. "Is this really you talking? You're normally the first in line to have a pop at people."

Tawna shrugged. "Maybe I'm softening in my old age."

"Anyway." Eve dragged out the word, making it sound much longer than three syllables. "Aren't we supposed to be opening presents?"

"Here, start with this one." Tawna handed me a shiny pink gift bag emblazoned with "It's A Girl!" in curly swirly script. "It's from me."

Layers of scrunched-up tissue paper rustled beneath my fingertips as I reached into the bag, reminding me of the lucky dip stalls at the summer fetes of my childhood.

Eventually the sensation of velvet tickling my fingers led me to the gift. As I pulled out a small soft-pink pouch Tawna couldn't hold back any longer.

"I know jewellery is more traditional for christenings than baby showers, but I couldn't resist. Every girl needs something sparkly to put on when she feels like she's lost her shine."

"That's certainly your motto," Eve quipped, nodding towards the square diamond earrings Tawna was wearing.

Tawna smiled as her hands reached up to her ears, fingering the precious jewels. "Too damn right."

The pouch opened to reveal a small silver bracelet, complete with one small charm. As I looked at it more closely I saw that it was a teddy bear.

"It's lovely, Tawna. Really beautiful."

Colour flushed to my friend's cheeks. "I hoped you'd like it. Johnny thought I was crazy buying something like this for a baby but I thought loads of people would be buying actual teddies and how many soft toys does a baby need?"

"Oi!" Eve said, pulling a face. "I bought a teddy."

"And I'll love it, as will this little one," I replied, rubbing my hand across my stomach. The squirm of movement twisting inside me suggested that baby agreed. "Anything from Auntie Eve will be much appreciated."

The teddy from Eve was opened next, followed by a breast pump, a changing mat, and enough clothes to give the old me a run for my money. My friends and family had gone to town, buying outfits for all occasions – dresses that were so tiny they looked like they'd be more suited to a doll than a miniature human, romper suits with gaping material to cover the bulge of a nappy, even a swimming costume, alongside copious amounts of vests and Babygros.

There was one present left, a gold box decorated with cerise spots.

"Last one," Eve said, passing me the box. It was lighter than I expected. "No label on it though."

"Maybe there's a note inside," Tawna suggested as I eased off the lid to be greeted by hundreds of pastel paper ribbons.

Pulling aside the shredded paper as carefully as possible, not wanting to make any more of a mess of Eve's carpet, I noticed a square piece of paper, baby pink.

"Found it," I said, waving the piece of paper aloft like Charlie Bucket as he found the final golden ticket, but when I lowered it to read who the gift was from I gasped. "Oh!"

"What is it?" Eve moved closer, peering over my shoulder to see what it was that had taken me aback.

"It's a gift voucher. For Jessie's mum's shop."

"That's fantastic," Tawna cooed. "Everyone knows how much you like the things she sells."

"For five hundred pounds."

"What? Who'd give you something like that?" Eve asked.

I shrugged, trying to downplay the chill running through me.

"Maybe it's from Jessie and Iris?" Eve suggested.

"Maybe," I echoed, "but they already gave me the baby sleeping bag."

"Or your work? A large amount of money like that could have been from a collection. Perhaps the bosses have been digging deep."

I held back a snort. The partners were all well known for their short arms and deep pockets. Many an hour had been spent listening to Jane complaining about the lack of a free bar at the Christmas do.

"Unlikely. Friday's my last day in the office and they're organising a leaving party for lunchtime. Marcie's making her speciality chilli."

"If anything will bring on labour it'll be Marcie's chilli," Tawna said, puffing out her cheeks. "I don't know what she puts in that stuff but it has a real kick."

"Ask at the shop, I'm sure they'll be able to tell you who paid for the voucher," Eve said, unable to let it go.

"I'm sure we'll find out soon enough." I put the voucher back in the box, burying it underneath the strands of lemon, lilac and rose-pink paper, not wanting to think about who was sending these gifts unsolicited. The whole thing gave me the heebie-jeebies. And how on earth was I going to explain such a generous gift to Max?

MAY

CHAPTER 33

The early summer sunshine blazed through the windows, the natural light that filled the room a relief after months of relying on the glare of strip lighting that usually filled the office. My workmates had gone to town decorating the staffroom, with pink and white balloons strung up from the ceiling, and banners stuck to the walls.

Spices from Marcie's chilli filled the air and everyone was in high spirits, singing along to the cheesy eighties playlist Jane had instructed Alexa to play. Even Mr Archer was up dancing to Culture Club, much to everyone's amusement.

"Phew, Marce, this is even hotter than last time." The roof of my mouth was aflame but even so I couldn't stop myself from adding more of the potent chilli to my jacket potato. "It's good though. Whatever you put in it makes it moreish."

Marcie tapped the side of her nose with her index finger. "Secret ingredient. I could tell you, but then I'd have to kill you."

"You're killing me anyway," Kath spluttered, water streaming from her bloodshot eyes. "I can hardly breathe."

"Oh, come on," said Jane, dryly. "After what you were telling me about the weekend I don't think you can make any comments about not being able to breathe."

I was aware my expression was puzzled, but all became clear as Jane continued.

"She's been telling me about her latest squeeze. Pat? Paddy?"

Kath shook her head. "Parky. Gabe Parker."

"No," I exclaimed, my fork hanging in mid-air as I took in the information. "Gabe Parker the electrician? I went to school with him. He was in my English class. All the girls fancied him. He won a national competition, something to do with woodwork, I think. Good with his hands."

"He still is," Kath said with a mischievous grin.

"What's that got to do with my chilli?" Marcie asked.

"Not the chilli, breathing," Kath corrected. "He's into ties and gags."

"I don't know if I want to hear this. He went out with my sister for a while."

"Maybe it's a new fetish, I don't know." Kath waved her hand dismissively. "All I can say is that he's very inventive when it comes to finding uses for cables."

I wasn't quite sure how to respond to that nugget of information, so was full of relief when Vernon Archer bellowed for everyone to quieten down so he could say a few words.

"Ah, Sophie." He smiled wistfully from underneath his bushy moustache. "Sophie, Sophie, Sophie. Where to start? You first arrived with us as a temp and didn't know what you were doing..."

I grimaced, colour flushing to my cheeks. During my first month I broke the photocopier four times and cut off callers when trying to transfer them to the right person. If I hadn't have needed the money I'd have quit.

"...but with Marcie as your line manager and the experience of Kath and Jane..."

"Less of the experience, makes me sound old," Kath quipped with a laugh.

"...Kath and Jane's support," he corrected, "you quickly became a part of the company, which is why we offered you a permanent contract. You're the baby of the work family, but now you are leaving us to have a baby of your own." He looked almost misty-eyed. "So from all of us here at Archer and Perkins I would like to wish you the very best for your maternity leave. Here's a little something from all of us."

He held out an envelope as everyone clapped.

"Make sure you bring the baby in to see us," said Dionne, one of the senior partners. "I want baby cuddles. It's a long time since mine were that small."

"Rest when you can," advised Jane. "When my two were little I'd sleep when they did to catch up on the hours I missed during the night."

"Take all the drugs they offer. You'll need them." That was Daisy from accounts.

As everyone tucked back into their jacket spuds and chilli and sipped at the Prosecco I'd brought in to celebrate (the non-alcoholic "no-secco" I'd bought for myself being surprisingly good), Mr Archer turned up the music and went back to his dad-dancing.

Daisy's words rang in my ears. The birth loomed large in my mind. Every night I'd wake in a cold sweat from nightmares where the baby would get stuck in the birth canal, or the one particularly weird dream where I'd given birth to a puppy. Up until this point I'd managed to put thoughts of labour to one side, instead focusing on the fun side of pregnancy – planning for baby's arrival and imagining how it would feel to hold this precious little person, half me, half Max, in my arms.

Forcing myself to smile, I accepted hugs and best wishes

from my colleagues, thanking them for the gift voucher they'd contributed to.

Daisy was hovering in the background but all I wanted to do was go and talk to her about giving birth. The antenatal classes had all been very positive, talking about the benefits of hypnobirthing and massage as well as covering the pain relief that was available to women during labour. I'd been lulled into a false sense of security.

Eventually, I couldn't hold back any longer.

"Daisy." I sidled up to her. "You said I should take all the drugs they offer during the birth."

"Definitely. Our Lori was back to back and weighed 10lb 4oz." I looked at Daisy's slim build, wondering how on earth she'd managed to grow a baby that size. "It was like trying to blow a bowling ball down a pea shooter," she added, the lovely imagery causing me to clamp my pelvic floor muscles together. "They started me off on a TENS machine." She laughed bitterly. "As if that was going to do anything. Then they gave me gas and air but that only took the edge off. I was begging for an epidural and it was the best thing ever. Couldn't feel a thing. Didn't stop me being ripped to shreds down below though. Had a third-degree tear and lost a lot of blood."

I could imagine how she felt as the colour drained from my cheeks. Why had I ever thought I'd be able to cope with the pain of giving birth? Daisy's hard as nails and she needed everything they could offer her, what made me think I would be able to manage with a few deep breaths and positive thoughts?

"Sounds nasty," I eventually managed, my mouth dry with anxiety.

"It was horrific. Matthias fainted when he saw how much blood there was. Out cold on the hospital floor. It took two midwives to scoop him back up."

There was something in Daisy's tone that I couldn't decipher.

Was she taunting me? I didn't think she was. We'd had our differences in the past but there had never been any spite.

"It was worth it all, of course. Lori is an absolute darling. Did I show you the picture of her from the gymnastics exhibition?" She pulled out her phone and scrolled, before thrusting the phone in my face.

Lori's pudgy face smiled out of the picture, the gap where her two front teeth had fallen out reminding me of one of Fagan's boys from *Oliver!* She was standing with her leg out to the side, a bright white streak of light breaking up the shot where the flash had reflected off the shiny purple leotard.

"She's growing up so quickly, she was just a baby when I started working here."

"They really do. Blink and you miss out on so much. My mum laughs at me for all the updates I post on Facebook but I don't want to miss out on anything. It seems two minutes since I was bringing her out of hospital, but she was six last month. Six! I can't believe it."

There wasn't much difference in her voice as she spoke about Lori to when she spoke about the trauma of giving birth. That's when it hit me what it was that I'd heard in her tone. It was pride.

&

Five o'clock rolled around quickly. My inbox was empty, my desk clear from the usual files that cluttered it.

"It's never been so tidy in here," Marcie joked. "If it's going to be like this when you're on maternity leave, I could get used to it."

I knew she was only teasing, my organised chaos being something all three of the women who I shared an office with found frustrating.

"It won't be the same without you." Kath clicked her mouse to close down her computer, the loud whirr of the system switching off followed by a decisive ping. "Who will I talk about *Married at First Sight* with if you're not here?"

"Maybe you can get Marcie and Jane to start watching," I said with a smile, knowing full well that neither of them enjoyed reality TV.

"Unlikely." Jane laughed. "But I agree with Kath, we'll really miss you. Don't be a stranger, we want to get to know your daughter."

"You won't be able to keep me away, I'll want to be showing her off."

"Come here," Marcie said, opening her arms wide. "Group hug."

And as the four of us wrapped our arms around each other, laughing at how much space my bump took up, I didn't feel the joy of escaping work that I'd expected. Instead, I felt quite sad.

CHAPTER 34

"She's talking nonsense. Do you really think people would go on and have second, third, fourth children if it was as bad as all that?"

I'd summoned Iris to the house after Daisy's conversation the previous week. The only thing I could focus on was that the baby had to come out, and soon. Pain wasn't my strong point. I'd cried my eyes out when I had my ears pierced, and that was as a twenty-year-old.

"I guess," I replied doubtfully.

"It hurts, I'm not going to lie and say it doesn't. And some births are more difficult than others." She paused to reach for a chocolate orange cookie from the plate in front of her. Thank heavens for the little bakery down the road.

"She mentioned third-degree tears. I didn't even know what one was until I googled and now I wish I hadn't."

"But you have to remember there are thousands of births every day where things run smoothly. Have you written up a birth plan?"

I shook my head. "Not yet. The midwife keeps telling me to do it but I don't know what I want."

"Do you know what you don't want?"

Iris's logic made sense. Why hadn't I thought of it that way?

"I don't want to be induced unless it's absolutely necessary, and I don't want to be lying on my back unless I choose to be. When the baby arrives, I want me or Max to be with her the whole time, even if she needs to be taken to another ward."

"See? You've already got ideas of how you want things to go. Write it down!"

My friend whipped a notepad out of her handbag with a flourish and passed it across the table to me, along with a stubby pencil.

"Isn't a birth plan meant to be more detailed than that?"

"Your birth, your birth plan," Iris replied firmly, before biting into the biscuit, quickly whipping her hand up to her chin to catch the crumbs that accompanied the snap as it broke.

Half an hour later I had a page full of notes about what I did and didn't want, everything from being open to the idea of an epidural if necessary to Eva Cassidy playing (her voice has always been a balm and if there was any time I needed comfort I figured it would be when trying to push out a baby).

"Do you feel better for writing down what you want?" Iris asked. "I remember writing my birth plan when we had Jude and Dana and afterwards I felt really..." she paused as she tried to conjure up the word, '...empowered, I suppose."

She looked at her daughter before reaching down to gently stroke the mottled skin of her cheeks.

"That's exactly it. I can't control how the birth will go, but this makes me feel stronger."

Strength was what I needed. The extra time on my hands since my last day at work had led to me overthinking everything.

Where most expectant mothers cleaned their house from top to bottom in a nesting frenzy prior to the birth, I was worrying myself sick over not only the birth but how I'd function on minimal sleep.

"I can't believe you'll be going through this in a matter of weeks," Iris said. "I loved giving birth. My body knew exactly what it needed to do. It's completely amazing."

"Were you nervous? In case it wasn't as smooth second time around, I mean."

"Not really," she says, tightly wrapping both hands around her mug. "Don't get me wrong, I'd have loved it if I had another complication-free birth, but the main thing was that both me and Dana were safe and well. Anything else was a bonus."

I compared Iris's outlook with Daisy's – the two were worlds apart. Daisy had approached it as though she was going into battle, wanting as many reinforcements as possible. Iris, on the other hand, was able to go with the flow. Neither was right, neither was wrong – they were just two different people with different views on childbirth. I was somewhere in the middle, not as relaxed as Iris but keen to go into it with an open mind. Part of me wanted to push my body to its limits, see exactly what it was capable of, but I wasn't scared to have drugs if needed. Having faith was what was important, trusting in the process.

My deep thoughts were interrupted by the chiming of the doorbell.

"I'd better see who it is," I said apologetically, although Iris didn't seem bothered as she waved me away and reached for a second biscuit.

The postwoman was obscured by the enormous box on the doorstep.

"Delivery!" she chirruped.

"You must have got the wrong house. We've not ordered anything this big."

"Sophie Drew, number five Anderson Green." She tapped the address label on the parcel authoritatively.

My heart dropped as the realisation hit home. Another "surprise".

I considered not accepting the parcel. If I didn't sign for it then the delivery couldn't be completed which would send a message to whoever was sending the packages that I didn't want or need them.

Curiosity won out though, and I found myself scrawling an illegible signature onto the woman's tablet with the lid-end of a Biro.

"Enjoy," she said, as she walked back along the drive.

The box was almost as tall as me and twice as wide. Getting it over the threshold and into the hallway was a struggle, especially as my bump had grown significantly over the past week. There was no finesse in my manoeuvres, and I could feel the stickiness under my armpits from the effort.

"Is everything all right?" Iris appeared in the hallway, biscuit in hand. "Woah." She took a step back when she saw the size of the box. "What's that?"

I shrugged. "No idea. Nothing I've ordered."

My friend pulled a grim face. "Another parcel from your unwanted admirer?"

"I don't know. I suppose Max could have bought something and not told me about it." My voice wasn't very convincing. "Although I don't think he'd dare."

"Soph, he pretty much bought a house without telling you, don't underestimate him."

"You're exaggerating. He's really good with money, since we moved we've got a spreadsheet for all the bills. He wouldn't make a big purchase without telling me, I'm sure of it."

"You'd better open it and see what's inside." Iris chewed on her biscuit. "You can't leave it there, it's blocking the hallway."

Tackling the package was an effort. The brown parcel tape alone was a humongous task, gripping, as it was, onto the box for dear life. Even with Iris to help it took five minutes to defeat the layer of cardboard.

"How many women does it take to open a cardboard box?" she joked, stepping aside as I opened the box. It was like a wardrobe as I peeled the doors back.

"Probably less than two if they had a pair of scissors." I'd laughed, trying to see what the bubble wrap sheath was protecting.

Between the pair of us we managed to wiggle the contents out, leaving the carcass of the box standing empty alongside what looked like a badly sculpted ice statue.

"What even is it?"

"I don't know," I answered drily, "I can't see through the five-inch-thick bubble wrap without my X-ray specs."

"Ha-ha." Iris retorted by sticking out her tongue. "You could always," she paused to gasp in mock horror, "open it. Or is that a radical idea?"

That was my cue to become the one pulling faces. "Very funny."

"Go on then." She picked at the end of a piece of Sellotape that was keeping the protective wrap in place. "Let's see what you've got."

It was like unwrapping an Egyptian mummy, rolling the packaging so that it was in a long cylinder, ready to reuse. It would be great for packaging up my Etsy sales.

"Let me see," Iris exclaimed, her excitement on a par with a small child on Christmas morning. "No way. No freaking way."

"It's a high chair." I took in the details of the wooden frame. Yes, it was a high chair but it looked like a work of art. The pale pine lines were modern yet had a classic, timeless style, and although in many ways it was simple it shrieked expensive.

"It's a Cavanagh Worcester," Iris replied, her voice breathy. "My absolute dream high chair. We nearly got one for Jude but couldn't justify it, even though they hold their value on the resale sites. They're not cheap, even second-hand."

"I've never heard of them. Should I have?"

My hand skimmed the cool wood. It was silky smooth, a flawless piece of design and impeccable quality.

"They're an Australian company, that's how I know about them. Huge over there but not as popular here yet. It's only a matter of time though, they're opening a distribution centre here in the UK. Jessie's mum was telling me all about it."

"But who would send me this? It's not even like I'll need it any time soon. It'll be six months before the baby starts on solids."

"If someone was sending me Cavanagh Worcester high chairs, I wouldn't be complaining."

"You're welcome to it," I said. "It could have been sent by any old weirdo."

"It's got to be someone you know, it wouldn't make sense otherwise. No one would spend that kind of money on a stranger. If I were you I'd just ask around more people and find out who it is."

"If only it was that easy. You wouldn't be saying that if you didn't know who it was sending you it," I replied, looking amongst the packaging to see if there was a note. Nothing. "I've asked everyone I can think of from my family, to my dick of an ex-boyfriend. No one is owning up."

"It's got to be. You just haven't asked the right person yet."

A dejected sigh escaped my lips. "Max'll hit the roof. Where can I put it so he doesn't see it?"

"Have you got a cellar?" Iris suggested. "Or in the garage?"

"The garage might be an idea, there are dust sheets from

when Max decorated the baby's room. I could hide it under those."

"Need a hand?" she asked, grabbing hold of one side of the high chair.

"Please." I smiled at my accomplice. "Max will be home from the carnival committee meeting in an hour."

CHAPTER 35

The carnival came around quickly, all Max and the committee's hard work coming to fruition. The dining room had become his office, a hub of organisation filled with stickers of flowers and stars to be stuck onto headbands for anyone who turned up hatless for the summer hat competition.

On the morning of the parade I woke early, giving up on the idea that I might find a comfortable position. Sleeping had gone by the wayside throughout the third trimester. I'd tried everything from extra pillows (both under my head and under my bump) to lavender-scented candles but nothing did the trick. Mum insisted it was nature's way of preparing me for the sleepless nights that lay ahead.

Max was sitting at the table trying to unpick the knots out of a string of bunting. From his under-his-breath mutterings I got the distinct impression it wasn't going well.

"Need a hand?" I asked, as he brought the string of flags closer to his face to unravel a particularly pesky knot.

"I'd love a coffee if you're putting the kettle on. I've been up since five panicking about all the things I need to get done."

"This event has been months in the planning. Everything

will be fine so long as you've got the chocolate for the kids. Don't sweat the small stuff, it's not worth it."

I leant down and placed a kiss on Max's forehead, and he put his hands either side of the dome of my stomach that doubled as our baby's home.

"Not long now, little one," he said. A shift from the little person in my belly caused him to laugh. "We can't wait to meet you."

"So long as she doesn't decide to make an appearance today, there's too much else we need to get done. We don't have the time to squeeze in having a baby on top of that."

"I think we're safe for a few more weeks, first babies are notoriously late, aren't they?"

"We're going to be late if we don't start getting organised. I'll make us a drink and crumpets, shall I? Then you can load up the car."

"What would I ever do without you?" Max put down the bunting. "I'm giving up on that," he added, pointing at the tangle of flags and ribbons on the table. "We've got plenty of decorations, I don't think anyone's going to miss one more string."

"I'm sure you're right," I replied, heading towards the kitchen. "Now go and put those chocolates in the car!"

The sun shone through the window as I filled the kettle and it was impossible to be anything but cheery. There was a sense of magic in the air which led me to believe it was going to be a good day.

The loud bubbling of the kettle reaching the boil (along with it rattling on its base) meant I didn't hear Max coming in. Besides, I was too busy humming S Club 7's "Reach".

"Sophie." His voice alone told me something was wrong, and when I spun around my boyfriend had a grim expression on his face. "Where did the high chair in the garage come from?"

Shit. I'd forgotten the chocolate had been stored in the cupboard at the back of the garage, right next to where Iris and I had hidden the high chair.

"It came the other day." My bottom lip trembled and I was aware of tears welling up behind my eyes. "Another present without a note."

"Why didn't you tell me?"

The look on his face was one of concern more than anything else.

"I didn't want to worry you. You were so angry when I told you about the gift voucher after the baby shower."

"Only because I don't know who's sending them. I'm not angry at you. I could never be angry at you."

"I thought you'd blame me, or think that I'd been spending crazy amounts of money on things for the baby."

"I know you wouldn't do that, Sophie. Most of the things you've been buying are second-hand and that high chair looks expensive."

"From what Iris was telling me it would have cost hundreds of pounds."

Max inhaled, teeth gritted together. A hissing sound followed.

"I'm sorry, I should have told you. I just knew you'd react like this."

"It doesn't make sense. The things they're sending are expensive. What they've sent probably costs more than I earn in a month. I don't get why anyone would spend that much, especially if they're not putting their name to it. It makes me uneasy."

"That's how I feel too. It's got to be someone we know well, because no one would spend that kind of money on an acquaintance."

Burden weighed heavy on my shoulders as I heaped instant

coffee into two mugs, added a splash of milk and then topped up with water before stirring.

"They've all been addressed to you rather than me," Max observed, "so it's got to be someone who's close to you. Are you absolutely sure it's not your family?"

"If they were going to give me anything they'd put their name to it. Once might have been a mistake, but this is going on and on."

"No long lost godmother who might be rolling in it?"

"Nope. My godmother died when I was little. I did wonder if it might be Norma. Her and Fred always thought of me as family. Maybe Fred put some money aside and she's putting it towards the baby."

"Or we could have been right before when we mentioned Darius," Max said, rolling his eyes. "This is exactly the kind of thing he'd do. Make himself out to be generous and me look like I can't support you and the baby."

"Honestly, I don't think it's him, and he knows that if I found out he was sending things that I'd make him take them all back and buy something for Summer instead."

"There's no one else I can think of," Max said, accepting the mug of coffee I handed him.

"Nor me. We'll just have to hope it becomes apparent when this little one arrives." I drew my hand across the hard swell of my belly. "Anyway, enough about that. Drink up and I'll pop some crumpets on, then we need to get out onto the green and make sure everything's set up. We can't let our new community down."

I slid two doughy crumpets into the toaster and slammed down the handle. However much I tried to forget it, I couldn't help wondering who was sending me the gifts and why.

But there was no time to dwell on it. The carnival wasn't going to organise itself.

"Look over there, Jude!" Iris was pointing at a giant lion high-fiving children as he walked across the green (It was Max in the costume, although no one would ever guess). "He's got chocolate! Let's get one for you and one for Dana."

"I don't think Dana's quite ready for chocolate yet," I said with a smile, my heart melting at the tiny baby sleeping in Iris's arms. "Maybe Mummy Jessie and Mummy Iris can share it instead."

"That's an idea I can get behind," Jessie replied, stifling a yawn. "These two tag-teamed all night long. I think we had twenty minutes sleep."

"You were snoring!" Iris retorted, but there was love in her eyes, a glow of pure contentment at her little family.

"Being a mum is hard work," Jessie's mum interjected, straightening the decorated hat her grandson was wearing, "but it's the best job in the world."

"Even better than running a baby boutique?" Jessie teased, knowing how proud her mum was of her little empire.

"Far better," she replied emphatically. "I love the shop but there's nothing like watching your children grow up."

We chatted for a while, pointing out the most elaborate headwear in the design a hat competition ("some people have way too much time on their hands," Iris chuntered) and watching the children decorating the shortbread biscuits Julie must have spent hours baking with brightly coloured icing and sugar strands.

Music filled the air, Max having roped in his friends Iain, Oz and Archie to play a set of popular hits and the cheery tunes along with the sunshine meant everyone was in high spirits. Although the carnival had originally been for residents of the green, word of the event had got around meaning there were hundreds of people enjoying themselves and raising money for the local hospice.

The party atmosphere was perfect and the children were having a wonderful time, which was exactly what it was in aid of. My mum manned a stall selling home-made candles and soaps, my latest favourite crafts, which went down a storm, and all proceeds were going to the charity.

My brother, hotdog in one hand, Noah's sticky palm in the other, called me over to the splat the rat stall, keen to point out the toy rodent.

"Remember that hamster you had when we were kids, the one that kept escaping. What did you call him again?"

"Hammy."

"That's the one. He looked like that toy rat."

I looked at the squashed piece of fluff being dropped down the long cardboard tube. "I'm insulted on Hammy's behalf. He was nothing like that!"

"Hamsters, mice, gerbils... they're all the same to me." Chantel wrinkled her nose in distaste. "They're not pets, they're pests. Wouldn't let any of our three have vermin in a cage."

Nick shovelled the last of his hotdog into his mouth before chasing after Noah, who was running towards a man selling helium balloons. My nephew was significantly quicker than my brother.

"What's the problem?" I looked my sister-in-law straight in the eye. "We've always got on. I don't only see you as Nick's wife, I think of you as my friend, but lately you've been really off with me. Anything I say, you say the opposite."

"No I don't."

"You're doing it now!" Exasperation raged inside me. "If you've got a problem with me, just say it. And if it's because the twins won't be the babies of the family anymore you've got nothing to worry about. Mum and Dad dote on those little girls, especially because of what they've been through."

Chantel inhaled sharply, the hiss of air audible even over the blaring music. "Do you really think that's what it is? That I'm scared your family won't love my children anymore?" She laughed, shaking her head. "You're wrong. So, so wrong."

"If it's not that, then what is it? You've got to admit things have been different between us lately. Even when me and Nick haven't been close I felt close to you. I don't get it."

"You wouldn't." Chantel stretched out her hand, gripped the pushchair and started rocking it back and forth.

"Then help me to understand."

She sighed. "Look, I know this is going to sound selfish, but I'm jealous. Jealous of how easy this has been for you." She gestured to my bump. "You've been able to enjoy being pregnant. You've made new friends, moved house. It's been a normal pregnancy." She paused, then looked down at the ground. "I'm not going to have that again, and my last experience of it was so horrific." She shuddered, and I recalled how worried we'd all been when we'd discovered the girls had twin-to-twin transfusion syndrome. It had been touch-and-go as to whether they'd both survive. "All I wanted was to enjoy being pregnant like I had with Noah, but instead I was bed-bound and scared."

"Why didn't you tell me? It's perfectly understandable that you'd feel that way, and I'm sorry if you've felt like I've been rubbing your nose in it. I thought I'd offended you in some way."

"I'm the one who should be sorry. I've been a bitch. We can't wait for our new niece to arrive, honestly. Me and Nick were only saying the other day how nice it'll be for Alicia and Imogen to have a cousin so close in age. When they're older they can share clothes and make-up and argue about boybands."

I laughed. "Give them a chance, that's a long way off yet."

"And we'll be waiting up at night when they're out clubbing, listening for them to get home."

"Stop it!"

She smiled softly. "Can you forgive me for how I've been?"

I reached out and placed my hand over hers. "Forgiven and forgotten."

CHAPTER 36

I was sipping on a freshly squeezed orange juice when Tawna and Johnny arrived.

"Look at you," Johnny said, greeting me with a kiss on each cheek. "Can't be long to go now."

"Due in three weeks," I confirmed, with a smile that was half excitement and half nerves.

"That's flown by, I bet you can't wait for her to arrive."

"We're just about ready now. Max finished painting the nursery last week and the midwife says that now we're at the thirty-seven week mark they class it as full term."

"Exciting times for you both. You're going to be great parents. I've seen what you're like around kids, Summer always worshipped the ground you walked on. I had to pull out all the stops as godfather extraordinaire to even try to compete with you."

"Ah, don't be daft. Summer thinks the world of you. You always spoil her rotten."

"She deserves it, she's an amazing little girl. Darius doesn't know how lucky he is to have her." I noticed him reach out for Tawna's hand and give it a squeeze. "We bought her a scooter the other week, didn't we?" he said, turning to look at my friend. "One with light up wheels that she'd been begging Nadia for. We got it the same day as we bought the high chair, didn't we Tawn?"

My jaw tightened. "High chair?"

"Yeah, the bike shop around the corner from The Baby Emporium was selling the scooters and I just knew we had to get one for Summer."

"Baby Emporium?" I parroted. My gaze fixed on Tawna, her eyes firmly focused on her designer sandals.

"It's a lovely little shop, Soph." Johnny carried on, clearly unaware of the tension between me and his wife. "Have you spent the voucher yet? I know it probably won't go far in a place like that but after all the fun me and Tawna have had in there buying things for your baby it only seemed fair that you should get to choose some items yourself."

"Not yet." I painted on a smile, not wanting to cause a scene in front of Johnny. This was something for me and Tawna to discuss between ourselves. "And I didn't have chance to thank you for all the presents. You really didn't have to, it's too much."

"No, I'm not having that," Johnny said, holding up his hand. "You're like family to Tawna and we wanted to treat you. We're really excited on your behalf. Our road to parenthood might not be so simple but that doesn't mean we can't be happy for you and Max."

My brain couldn't keep up with the conversation. Tawna and Johnny had bought all the gifts? So one of my oldest friends has been lying to me for months? And what did Johnny mean about their road to parenthood not being simple?

"We're very grateful," I forced, "we can't thank you enough."

Tawna refused to catch my eye, instead looking with intent at the group of toddlers adding stickers and sequins to cardboard headbands. She looked like she was about to burst into tears.

"Johnny," I placed a hand on his arm, "can I borrow your wife for a moment? There's something I need to talk to her about."

"Be my guest," Johnny replied with a shrug and a smile. "I'll go and see if Max needs any help running the dancing competition. He'll be hard to miss in that costume."

He kissed his wife's cheek before heading off, leaving me and Tawna alone.

The only problem was, I didn't quite know where to begin.

"I know what you're thinking," Tawna started but I swiftly cut her short as I weaved through the people milling on the green to the seclusion of my back garden.

"You don't have a clue what I'm thinking."

My jaw was tight, teeth gritted together so hard that my words sounded slurred. Rage fizzed in my chest. How could Tawna do this? She knew how uncomfortable I was about the gifts but yet she still kept sending them. The anger remained deep in my core, but there was more to it than that. My emotions were so raw that they physically hurt.

"Why, Tawna? Did you get off on throwing Johnny's money around? We might not be loaded like you, but we don't need your handouts."

"It wasn't like tha—"

"I don't want to hear it. You've always got an excuse, haven't you? Like you've got a divine right to do whatever you want and damn the consequences. It was the same with your hen do, you just got an idea in your head and booked it without even asking me and Eve. But everyone always drops everything for you, don't they? And you smile your little smile and get away with it. Every. Bloody. Time."

The anger fuelled me. I was a long way from finishing saying my piece, in fact I was only just finding my stride.

"You don't have a clue what it's like for the rest of us. All your life you've had everything you ever wanted given to you on a plate. When we're all working, you're off having spa days and getting your hair done. You can't imagine what it's like dragging yourself out of bed every day and doing the same monotonous tasks over and over and over, just to earn a living." I pause for breath, but not long enough for a gawping Tawna to interrupt. "When the presents first started arriving it was unnerving. I thought they were from Darius! How do you think Max felt when he thought my ex was the one sending things for our baby? It caused so much tension. Then the presents that arrived were more and more expensive. What made you think sending things without so much as a note was a good idea? Oh, I forgot, you don't think, do you? You rush on ahead and do whatever you want, fuck everyone else."

Tawna gasped, aware that I rarely resort to swearing, let alone the f-bomb.

"I told you time and time again that the gifts were scaring me. I asked you outright if it was you sending them and you said no! You lied to me. You're supposed to be one of my best friends but you lied to me. Some friend."

A twinge from my stomach caused me to catch my breath, like the stitch I used to get during cross country at school, but it disappeared almost before it began.

"I'm s-s-sorry. I n-n-never meant for it to go this far."

Tears streamed down Tawna's cheeks, leaving dull trails in their wakes. Seeing Tawna looking anything less than her usual immaculate self gave me pause for thought, but not for long.

The lies, the deceit – a few crocodile tears weren't going to be enough to win me around this time.

"What were you thinking? Were you trying to freak me out? Because that's what it feels like."

"No," Tawna wailed, the tears coming faster than before. "I was trying to make myself feel better."

I rolled my eyes. "Of course you were. It's always Tawna, Tawna, Tawna." My tone was mocking, cruel, but I couldn't help myself. She'd let me down.

"We've been trying for a baby," she blurted, her mascara-lined face etched with pain. "Ever since the wedding." She closed her eyes, taking a deep breath before exhaling through pursed lips. "I had an ectopic pregnancy."

My hand instinctively wrapped my stomach, as though doing so would protect my baby from harm. A cramp pulsed through my belly, a tight taut pull that caused bile to rise in my throat.

"Oh, Tawna, I had no idea."

"Why would you? I didn't tell anyone." She laughed sadly. "We'd wanted to get to the twelve-week scan before telling everyone, but we didn't make it that far. Two happy weeks we had. Two weeks where me and Johnny saw ourselves as Mummy and Daddy."

The all-encompassing rage faded. It would have been impossible for it not to, faced with one of my oldest friends in such agony.

"You should have told me," I said softly, my own eyes filling with tears of secondary sadness. "No one should have to go through that alone."

"How could I tell you? You had your own pregnancy to celebrate. It wouldn't have been right."

"But I could have helped you. You must have been in hospital? I could have come to visit."

Guilt caused my stomach to spasm once more.

"I had Johnny, and my mum. And Eve was an absolute star."

I swallowed. "Eve knew?"

"It wasn't about keeping secrets from you. I didn't want to worry you. You'd already been scared something would go wrong after Chantel's pregnancy with the twins, I couldn't bring myself to tell you."

My heart ached for her, for all the hurt she'd held inside to protect me. That was love in action, a true sacrifice.

"We've always shared everything." I reached out and held her hand between mine. "I wish I'd been there to support you when you needed me the most. You must have been heartbroken."

She nodded. "That's why I bought you all the things. They were meant to be a nice surprise. We bought the blanket the day me and Johnny found out we were expecting." She swallows. "We bought two. One for your baby and one for…"

I squeezed her hand, unable to find the words.

"Two weeks later I woke up in the middle of the night, the pain was like nothing else. I was screaming in agony. Johnny was terrified, he thought I was dying. I thought I was dying. We raced to A&E. Johnny went through every red light. By the time we got to the hospital I was delirious. People talk about seeing stars but I never knew what they meant until that day."

Emotion took over and I had to wrap her in my arms. She'd gone through so much, lost so much. It was unthinkable.

"Go on. If you want to."

"When they found out I was pregnant they took me for a vaginal ultrasound. I was convinced it was a miscarriage and although I couldn't see the screen I knew something was wrong. Even though I couldn't focus I could see the sonographer's face and it was obvious it wasn't good news. That's when she told us, the baby was growing in my fallopian tube. They took me straight into surgery." Her voice cracked as she added, "They gave me an anaesthetic. When they knocked me out I was pregnant, when I woke up I'd lost a baby and a tube. Sometimes they can save them, but mine was too damaged."

"I'm so, so sorry. And I'm sorry if being around me has upset you. It can't have been easy for you."

"No, no." Tawna shook her head vehemently. "We're so happy for you and Max. It was a horrible experience but that doesn't stop us being excited for you. And I'm so excited, Soph." She placed her hand on my stomach, the rock-hard bump of my baby's bottom jutting out from beneath my ribcage. "That's why we bought you all those presents. We wanted to spoil you, but knew you wouldn't accept them. If we can't buy things for our own baby, we can at least buy them for yours. You've always been like a sister to me, and I want to be the best honorary auntie to your little one that I can possibly be. And one day maybe she'll have an honorary little cousin to play with. The hospital said that even though I've only got one tube there's a good chance we'll get pregnant again if we keep trying because there was no sign of damage to my ovaries."

It was impossible to be angry after hearing her story. The gesture had been misplaced, but it was carried out with love.

"And you will be."

We sat for a moment, heads leaning into each other's in a way they had so many times over the years, the thrilled cheers of children finding the chocolates Max had painstakingly hidden the soundtrack to our hug.

CHAPTER 37

"Argh!" I untangled myself from my friend and bent double, rocking backwards and forwards, the agony causing me to grit my teeth together.

A hand smoothed my hair, the same way it had when I'd been suffering horrendous hangovers or the worst heartbreaks.

"Are you all right, Soph? Is it the baby? Do you think it's coming?"

All the anxieties about giving birth swarmed my mind. Could these be Braxton-Hicks, the "warm up" contractions as the midwife had called them? Or was this the real deal? I didn't know, but one thing I was sure of was that I needed Max beside me.

"I don't know," I replied, taking huge gulps of the air. As if breathing hadn't been difficult enough with the baby taking up so much space, crushing my internal organs until even climbing up off the sofa was a mammoth effort. "Get Max. Please. Get Max."

Tawna withdrew her phone from her pocket and I put all my energy into keeping my breathing steady.

My face naturally contorted into a grimace, a noise not

dissimilar to a moo escaping through my gritted teeth. All I wanted was to know that Max was on his way.

"Pick up, pick up," Tawna muttered as she tapped her foot impatiently.

It seemed like an age before I heard her talking and relief coursed through me. He was coming. Max would be with me and everything would be okay.

Her voice was low and, with every ounce of my concentration focussed on breathing, I couldn't hear what she was saying.

"Is he coming? Please say he's coming…"

Tawna rubbed the small of my back with the heel of her hand as I rocked back and forth on my knees. It hurt. It hurt so much.

Eventually the hum of her voice faded.

"Is he coming?" I repeated. "Is Max on his way?"

"Johnny's going to find him," she said soothingly, the circular motion not stopping for a second. "He'll be here soon."

My veins filled with panic, the adrenaline racing through me multiplying. "Why isn't he answering his phone?"

"He's still dressed up and the costume doesn't have pockets. Johnny's looking after his phone and wallet for him."

"I think this is it." I winced. "I think I'm dying."

Tawna laughed, but it was a kind laughter. "I don't think you're dying, but I do think your daughter wants to be part of the celebrations. Johnny's fetching Max now to take you to the hospital. You don't want to give birth here, in your back garden."

An absurd thought rushed through my head, an image of giving birth underneath the apple tree. But that wasn't in the plan me and Iris had put together with painstaking effort. I needed to be at the hospital, with midwives and anaesthetists and consultants on hand.

My body contorted as another agonising wave hit. I'd

expected a gentle easing in of contractions, not a full-on assault. It was like Serena Williams swinging her racquet against my stomach, at full pelt, repeatedly.

"I'm here, Sophie," my friend cooed, the rhythmic rubbing of my back not missing a beat. "You're doing great. Deep breaths. You've got this."

Hearing Tawna's voice, so familiar and reassuring, relaxed me. The contractions still felt like they were splitting my insides in two, but my friend's words rooted me in the present and reminded me of the end goal.

All I could do was focus on breathing in through my nose and out through my mouth, just the way the midwife had explained at antenatal classes.

In for four, out for four. In for four, out for four. It became a mantra.

After what felt like hours, but may have only been minutes, Johnny called over the fence.

"Come on, we need to get you to the hospital."

Tawna eased me to my feet as I grumbled, my whole being creased in pain. The sensation was unlike anything I'd experienced before, throbbing through every inch of my body before dulling to a low ache, only to surge again a few minutes later. Each step was a gargantuan effort.

When we reached the driveway all my breathing efforts went out of the window. There was no sign of Max, nor his car. Instead we were greeted by Johnny's black convertible XKR Jaguar.

"Where's Max? I thought he was coming? I can't do this without him." Hysteria rose within me at the thought of labouring without my boyfriend at my side.

"He's going to meet us at the hospital," Johnny explained as he opened the car door. "Come on, let's go."

I climbed into the back seat in an ungainly manner, cursing as the seat belt cut into me.

Breathe, Sophie, breathe.

Another wave hit and my hands gripped the seats, my nails threatening to puncture the buttercream upholstery as a wetness spread between my legs. At first I thought I'd peed myself, minor incontinence being one of the many unwelcome side effects I'd experienced throughout pregnancy, but it didn't take long to realise it wasn't that. There was too much fluid.

My waters had broken, all over Johnny's beautiful leather seats.

CHAPTER 38

By the time we arrived at the maternity unit, I was beginning to wonder how much more I could take. I was beyond the limits of my pain threshold and the fear of the unknown combined with the searing pain had me in tears. Not to mention that my spotty dress and pants were soaked through – when the midwife instructed I sit in a wheelchair to be taken down to the labour suite I was reluctant. No wonder babies cry when they've got a wet nappy. Not even the painful contractions were enough of a distraction.

"I can't do this. You'll have to give me a caesarean," I told the midwife as she wheeled me along the sterile corridors.

"Let's get you comfortable first, then I'll examine your cervix to see how dilated you are."

Comfortable. Was she joking? I couldn't imagine ever being comfortable again.

Transitional phase. That's why I'd been almost delirious with pain and begging for any and every drug they could offer. In the end I'd settled on gas and air, sucking on the mouthpiece like an addict who'd been without their fix for months having their first longed-for hit.

"You're doing so well, Sophie," the midwife encouraged. "And you're fully dilated so with your next contraction you can give a gentle push if you feel the urge."

The sensation was just like when I needed a poo, a heavy bearing-down low in my pelvis.

"Can't," I said, briefly detaching my lips from the plastic before inhaling deeply and getting another hit of Entonox. The head rush was immense. "Need Max. On his way."

Tawna and the midwife shared a look.

"Johnny's still trying to get hold of him," Tawna admitted. "Johnny's taken the car and gone back to the green so I'm sure they'll be here soon."

An overwhelming desire to strain came over me, and I understood what people meant when they said their body took over in labour. There was no other option but to push.

Waiting for Max to arrive was impossible, the baby was ready to make her appearance.

"That's it. If the contraction's still there, keep pushing."

Push.

Pant.

Push.

Pant.

Push.

Pant.

The midwife was the conductor and I was ready to take her lead, just so long as I could keep hold of the gas and air. Chewing on the plastic at the height of each contraction was getting me through.

Sweat clung to my hairline, errant beads dripping down my forehead. Giving birth was a gruelling workout. Who knew?

"Fantastic. I can see the top of Baby's head. If you reach down you can feel it yourself."

Another wave crashed through me before I had the chance, a caustic sting burning as I pushed. Iris had warned me about this. Crowning. The ring of fire. If someone had told me they'd taken a match to my foof and set it alight I'd have believed them.

"Keep going, that's it," the midwife cheered.

"I can see her hair!" Tawna exclaimed. "It's fair, just like Max's."

As though summoned, the door burst open, tears of relief streaming down my red-hot face as Max dashed in. I knew that whatever happened it would be okay once Max was by my side. Even if he was dressed in a furry lion costume. At least he'd had the foresight to take the head off. Thank heavens for small mercies.

"I'm sorry, I'm so sorry. I almost missed it."

He reached for my one free hand (no way was I letting go of the drugs at such a crucial moment).

"You're here now," the midwife reassured him, "and just in time, I'd say. A few more pushes like the last one and your daughter will be here."

"Look at the baby's hair, Max." Even in my hazy state I recognised the awestruck expression on Tawna's face.

Without loosening his grasp, he leant to look between my legs, the very first glimpse of his daughter. He gasped, cupping his hand over his mouth as he swallowed down his emotion.

"I can see her, Sophie. She's ready to meet us."

As he spoke I pushed with all my might, and the midwife cheerfully said, "That's the head. Three twenty-four pm."

I dropped the gas and air onto the bed, putting my hand down between my legs to be met by a solid, sticky mass. Our daughter, on the cusp of the universe.

One final push and a long, dull bellow later, she slithered into the world, welcomed by three tearful adults and one midwife following the protocols required of the situation.

"Baby girl delivered, three twenty-six pm."

A caterwaul followed, fractured cries from the tiny being echoing around the room.

Everything happened in a blur until a bundle of blankets with a bright red face peeping out was placed in my arms.

"Our daughter," Max whispered, stroking her hair with the finest touch. "Our perfect, perfect baby."

"Congratulations," Tawna said, wiping a tear from her eyes. "I'll leave you three to get to know each other." I blew her a kiss and mouthed a "thank you".

The midwife remained in the corner of the room, filling in paperwork as our little family floated on air.

"You were amazing, Sophie. Absolutely amazing."

"She's amazing." Waxy vernix covered her face, lips in a perfect rosebud pout. "What do you think? Is she a Scarlett?"

Max nodded.

"Scarlett Oakley-Drew," he said thoughtfully. "Sounds perfect to me. Just like Sophie Oakley-Drew does. What do you think?"

"Are you asking what I think you're asking?"

Max looked deep into my eyes, the love evident. "I've wanted to ask you for months but it's never been the perfect moment. I even got you a ring. It's been in my bedside drawer since we moved. This feels like the right time to ask though. Like it's the start of something. Marry me, Sophie. Make me the happiest man alive."

I held Scarlett closer to me, warmth radiating from her body to mine.

"Yes." I laughed, joy bursting within me.

And the three of us embraced, in our blissful state, safe in the belief that the future would be golden.

THE END

Sophie Drew will return...

ACKNOWLEDGEMENTS

A second *Sophie* book and one which would never have come about but for all these wonderful people!

Huge thanks to –

The team at Bloodhound Books, with special thanks to Betsy Reavley, Tara Lyons, Maria Slocombe and Morgen Bailey.

Philippa Ashley, Mary Jayne Baker, Sarah Bennett, Rachel Burton, Brigid Coady, Miranda Dickinson, Rachel Dove, Lynsey James, Josie Silver, Linda Stacey, Keris Stainton, Inky Willis and all the Wordcount Warriors, A***-Kickers and Beta Buddies for your continued support and friendship.

The book blogger/vlogger/bookstagram community for always championing commercial women's fiction.

All my friends, especially those I've made through being a mum – Lydia Peto, thanks for everything.

My family, for loving me and supporting me even when I'm unravelling.

Most of all, thank *you* for following Sophie's journey. You are golden.

Katey Lovell, Sheffield, June 2021